# "The plan?"

"The press are going to swarm around you like hornets, so you need to go to ground. Immediately."

Elspeth gripped the back of an oak chair to steady her suddenly trembling legs. "The press?"

"The paparazzi. One whiff of this and you'll be hounded for an exclusive tell-all interview. But I should warn you against giving one."

Elspeth swallowed. The thought of the press hounding her, chasing her, thrusting microphones and cameras in her face terrified her. "I would never do that."

One dark eyebrow winged upward. "I'm afraid I can't afford to believe you, so I will be accompanying you until this blows over."

Elspeth gawked at Mack. Had she heard him correctly? "Accompanying me? Accompanying me where?"

"To a secret hideaway."

"You're...kidnapping me?" Her eyes were so round they threatened to pop out of her head. Could this farce get any more ridiculous?

He gave a light laugh. "Ever the drama queen. No, I'm giving you a choice. Either you come with me willingly or I leave you to face the destruction of your reputation and quite possibly your career."

## The Scandalous Campbell Sisters

*It started with a switch!*

Twins Elspeth and Elodie Campbell may be identical, but looks aside, they couldn't be *more* different. So superconfident Elodie's idea that they switch places—at a society wedding no less!—has shy Elspeth on edge. Library archivist Elspeth would do anything for Elodie... But standing in for her supermodel sister? It's a recipe for disaster—surely! Add in a Scottish tycoon and an ex-fiancé... Well, life is about to get complicated for Elspeth and Elodie!

Meet the Campbell sisters in...

Elspeth and Mack's story

*Shy Innocent in the Spotlight*

Available now!

And look out for Elodie and Lincoln's story

*A Contract for His Runaway Bride*

Coming soon!

# Melanie Milburne

---

## SHY INNOCENT IN THE SPOTLIGHT

Recycling programs
for this product may
not exist in your area.

ISBN-13: 978-1-335-56901-1

Shy Innocent in the Spotlight

Harlequin Enterprises ULC
22 Adelaide St. West, 40th Floor
Toronto, Ontario M5H 4E3, Canada
www.Harlequin.com

**Printed in U.S.A.**

**Melanie Milburne** read her first Harlequin novel at the age of seventeen, in between studying for her final exams. After completing a master's degree in education, she decided to write a novel, and thus her career as a romance author was born. Melanie is an ambassador for the Australian Childhood Foundation and a keen dog lover and trainer. She enjoys long walks in the Tasmanian bush. In 2015 Melanie won the HOLT Medallion, a prestigious award honoring outstanding literary talent.

### Books by Melanie Milburne

### Harlequin Presents

*Billionaire's Wife on Paper*
*The Return of Her Billionaire Husband*
*The Billion-Dollar Bride Hunt*

### Once Upon a Temptation

*His Innocent's Passionate Awakening*

### Secret Heirs of Billionaires

*Cinderella's Scandalous Secret*

### Wanted: A Billionaire

*One Night on the Virgin's Terms*
*Breaking the Playboy's Rules*
*One Hot New York Night*

Visit the Author Profile page
at Harlequin.com for more titles.

To all the nut allergy sufferers out there. Your daily battle to stay safe is such a challenge that often goes unrecognized. And a special thank-you to Emily Payne for describing what it feels like to experience both anaphylaxis and its treatment. And here I was thinking being gluten intolerant was bad! xxxx

# CHAPTER ONE

ELSPETH STARED AT her twin sister in heart-stopping, skin-prickling, I-can't-believe-what-I'm-hearing alarm. 'You want me to do *what*?'

Elodie rolled her eyes as if it were a competitive sport she was trying to win a gold medal in. 'It's not like you've never been a bridesmaid before. This will be—'

'The one and only time I was a bridesmaid, the bride didn't show up,' Elspeth said with a speaking look. 'Or have you completely erased jilting Lincoln Lancaster from your memory?'

Elodie gave a dismissive wave of her hand. 'Oh, that was years and years ago. Everyone's forgotten about that now.' She leaned forward on the sofa with a beseeching puppy-dog look in her blue eyes. 'So, will you do it? Will you stand in for me, just for the wedding rehearsal, in the Highlands of Scotland?

You've always said you'd like to see where our ancestors came from. I'll be back in time for the wedding and we'll do a quick switch and you can leave by a back door and no one will ever know a thing.'

'But why can't you be there yourself? What's so important that you can't be there for your friend the whole weekend?'

'Sabine is not actually a close friend as such,' Elodie said with a side note of cynicism in her tone. 'I know for a fact I've only been invited to be her bridesmaid because of my fame as a lingerie model. She likes to surround herself with influencer types and apparently she sees me as one. I've only met her a handful of times, which is why you and I switching places will work so well.'

Elspeth cast her gaze over her twin's beautifully made-up face, her professionally styled hair and perfectly manicured hands. They might be identical twins but they lived in entirely different worlds. Elodie's world was exotic and expansive and exciting. Elspeth's world was small and secure and safe...well, as safe as anyone could be who lived with a life-threatening peanut allergy. Elspeth wanted to help her sister, they were close and had always had each other's back, but they hadn't switched places since they were kids. But a society wedding was a big deal. She wasn't great at mingling, hated small talk and was painfully shy when out of her natural environment.

But then, the chance to visit Scotland, the birthplace of their ancestors, was tempting—especially without her overprotective mother tagging along as she did the last time Elspeth tried to have a weekend away. Talk about embarrassing.

*But...*

Her life to date had been a series of 'buts' and 'what ifs'. She had missed out on so many activities her peers took for granted. Her world had shrunk while her sister's had expanded. Their mother's fear for Elspeth's survival since infancy had become pathological. But, to be fair, there had been a few horrendous moments during her childhood and adolescence when she had accidentally come into contact with peanuts. Her first proper date being particularly notable. One kiss and she had to be rushed to hospital in a sirens-screaming, lights-flashing ambulance. Not fun. Travelling anywhere outside her safety zone was fraught with potential danger. What if she ran out of EpiPens or couldn't get to a hospital in time? What if she made a complete and utter fool of herself? 'I don't know...'

Elodie bounced off the sofa and placed her hands on her hips, her expression etched in stern lines of reproof only an older sister by ten minutes could pull off. 'See? You *always* do that.'

Elspeth looked at her in puzzlement. 'Do what?'

'You limit yourself. You say no when deep down you really want to say yes.' Elodie ran a hand through her long curly mane of red-gold hair. 'You do it because of Mum always being so overprotective of you. But you need to get out more, Els. You have to prove to Mum you can do stuff on your own and this is a perfect chance to do it. You have no life other than working at the library. You haven't been on a date since you were eighteen, for God's sake. And apart from work, you spend most of your time alone. Don't you want to see how the other half lives for a change? Have some fun? Be daring and spontaneous?'

Elspeth knew there was an element of truth in her twin's observation—a truth she had been avoiding facing for quite some time. Her world was small, too small, and lately she had been feeling the walls of her tiny world closing in on her even more. But that didn't mean stepping into her twin's sky-high party-girl shoes for twenty-four hours in the Highlands of Scotland was a wise or sensible thing to do. 'But you haven't answered my question. What's so important that you can't be at the wedding rehearsal yourself? Why the need for the crazy subterfuge?'

Elodie lowered her hands from her hips and sat back on the sofa opposite Elspeth. She clasped her hands between her bent knees, her eyes sparkling with barely contained excitement. 'Because I have a top-secret meeting in London about possible financial backing for my own designs. You know how desperately I want to launch my own label? Well, this could be my big chance to do it.' Her expression suddenly became as sombre as an undercover operative talking to a fellow agent. 'My *only* chance to do it. But I don't want to compromise my current contract if word got out that I was thinking of leaving. I want the finances done and dusted before I hand in my resignation.'

Elspeth could understand her twin's desire to leave the world of lingerie modelling behind. She, personally, as an introvert, could not think of anything more terrifying than strutting down a catwalk in just knickers and a bra or a bikini. But her extroverted twin had up until recently seemingly enjoyed the limelight, lapping up the fame and regular travel to exotic locations for photo shoots. When Elodie uploaded a new bikini on her Instagram account, the sales went through the stratosphere. Elspeth, on the other hand, didn't have any social-media platforms, nor did she have any bikinis. She was a one-piece, keep-her-life-private type of girl.

Would it hurt to step out of her comfort zone for twenty-four hours? To switch places with her twin just long enough to see what life was like on the other side? It wasn't as if she were going on a photo shoot for her twin. It wasn't even for the actual wedding, just the rehearsal. 'Is there anyone else you know who's going to the wedding? I mean, more intimately than the bride?'

Elodie reached for her drink on the coffee table, her eyes not quite meeting Elspeth's. 'One or two casual acquaintances maybe.'

Elspeth sat up a little straighter in her seat, a chill running down her spine as if a blast of cold wind had blown through the window straight off the top of the Cairngorms. 'But what if someone realises it's not you?'

'How will anyone know it's not me?' Elodie asked. 'You were the one who insisted I never mention I had an identical twin when I started modelling. The most I've ever said in an interview is I have a younger sister, but I didn't say how much younger. Your privacy will remain intact because everyone will think it's me, not you. And because you're not on social media, and you were home-schooled, there are no photos of us together, no one is likely to make the connection. Our secret will be safe. Trust me.'

'But what about your wedding?' Elspeth said. 'Some photos of the wedding party were leaked online, remember? And every-one at the wedding had a go at me because they thought I must have known you were going to pull the plug on Lincoln. I'm sure I was referred to as your twin in at least a couple of press releases.'

Elodie chewed at her lower lip for a brief moment, her smooth brow furrowing slightly. But then her expression went back to its I've-got-this-covered mode. 'That was so early in my career, no one will remember it. Lincoln was far more famous than me back then.'

'But that's exactly my point. What if some-one did a little research? Once online, always online, remember?'

'You're worrying too much.'

Elspeth had good reasons for not wanting

any media exposure as a result of her sister's career. Elodie had always played on her looks, always loved being the centre of attention, always loved working the room. Elspeth had done the opposite—always downplaying her physical assets so as to avoid the attention her twin craved. Elspeth could not bear the thought of dozens of paparazzi chasing her down the street, thrusting numerous camera lenses in her face, potentially mistaking her for her twin. Could not bear the thought of her private life being made fodder for gossip magazines.

Could not bear to be compared to her vivacious twin and found lacking.

Elspeth wasn't charming and vivacious, she wasn't a social butterfly, she was a moth.

But...the prospect of twenty-four hours pretending to be her twin did trigger a strange sense of excitement in her blood. It was a chance to step out of her cocoon of cotton wool. The cocoon their mother had wrapped her in since her first anaphylactic reaction as a two-year-old. She wasn't two any more. She was twenty-eight and tired of being mollycoddled by her mum. Moving into her own flat a month ago had been the first step towards greater autonomy. Maybe this would be another chance to prove to her mother she could move about in the world without putting herself in mortal danger.

'Okay…' Elspeth mentally crossed her fingers. 'Let's do it.'

'Yay!' Elodie flung her arms around her and almost lifted her off the floor in a bone-crushing hug. 'Thank you. Thank you. Thank you. I'll never be able to thank you enough for doing this.' She planted a smacking kiss to Elspeth's cheek. *'Mwhah.'*

Elspeth grimaced and peeled her twin's octopus-like arms from around her body. 'You'd better save your thanks until the gig is over. I don't want you to jinx me.'

'You'll be brilliant. Remember that time we switched on one of our access visits to Dad when we were ten? He never guessed the whole weekend.'

'Yes, well, that says more about Dad than it does our acting ability, even if you did do rather a fantastic job of pretending to be a bookworm.' It was an amazing feat on her twin's part, given Elodie had dyslexia and avoided reading whenever she could. Elspeth, on the other hand, had been reading since she was four and, as she'd been home-schooled by her mother due to her allergy, her life had always revolved around books and reading. And now, her work as a library archivist was a dream career, one where she was paid to do what she loved.

Elodie laughed. 'I was bored out of my brain and I nearly went cross-eyed trying to make sense of the words. Give me a juicy gossip mag any day.'

'Even when you're in one?'

Elodie's eyes sparkled like fairy lights. 'Especially when I'm in one.'

Now it was Elspeth's turn to roll her eyes and she suppressed a shudder. 'Eek. I can think of nothing worse.'

Mack MacDiarmid surveyed the wedding preparations taking place on his country estate, Crannochbrae, with a critical eye. Weddings weren't his thing but his younger brother, Fraser, wanted to be married at home, so no expense was being spared to make it a wedding to remember. The fact his troubled brother was finally settling down was definitely something to celebrate. Mack had spent way too many years worrying about Fraser's tendency to act impulsively and irresponsibly, but Fraser's fiancée, Sabine, had come along at the right time and Mack hoped her stable influence over time would be the making of his brother. It had certainly worked miracles so far, but Mack's inner cynic was holding its breath.

The garden where the service was to take place had never looked better. The wisteria walk was in full bloom, the sweet fragrance filling the air. The castle had been cleaned from top to bottom—everything sparkled, everything shone, everything glowed. The guests' rooms had been aired and made up and the kitchen was full of catering staff busily preparing the food for the weekend. Even the notoriously capricious summer weather had decided to cooperate. It was cloudy today, but tomorrow's forecast looked promising—bright and sunny. There was a storm predicted for later in the evening, but the wedding ceremony would be well and truly over by then.

Sabine was darting here and there, double-checking everything was going according to plan, which was supposed to be the highly paid wedding planner's job, but Sabine wasn't the sort of person to relinquish control to someone else. Not that Mack could talk—he had triple-checked everything too. He wanted his brother's wedding to go smoothly, which meant he was issued with the job of keeping an eye on Elodie Campbell, one of the bridesmaids, in case she caused trouble. Exactly what trouble she might cause was anyone's guess. Fraser had been a little cagey about his connection with Elodie but Mack had checked her out online and drawn his own conclusions. She was a stunning lingerie model with more followers on social media than had some Hollywood celebrities. She had jilted her fiancé at the altar seven years ago and had developed a reputation as a party girl ever since. He knew from experience party girls were notoriously unpredictable but he was well prepared.

Mack had made it his life's work to be well prepared. Losing his father to suicide at the age of sixteen had forced him to never leave things to chance, to always be vigilant, to tick all the boxes, to do what needed to be done, to say what needed to be said, when it needed to be said.

To *always* be in control.

Mack turned to look back at the house and caught sight of a red-gold cloud of hair and a pale oval face looking down at him from one of the guest rooms upstairs. He had never met her in person but he had seen enough photos of her in the press to recognise Elodie Campbell. An understated version, that was. She was wearing a cream silk wrap and, with her wildly curly hair pulled up in a makeshift knot on her head, she had an old-world air that was utterly captivating. She could easily have been one of his ancestors travelling through time to pay a ghostly visit. He lifted a hand in a wave but she darted away from the window so quickly he blinked a couple of times, wondering if he had indeed imagined her standing there. He shrugged and continued on his way. Perhaps the stunningly beautiful Elodie Campbell didn't like being seen without her make-up on.

Elspeth leaned back against the wall of her bedroom and clutched a hand to her chest where her heart was bouncing up and down like a yo-yo on an elastic string. She was in no doubt the man she had seen just now was Mack MacDiarmid. Elodie had shown her a photo on her phone of Fraser and Sabine, and had briefed her about a number of other guests, but told her zilch about Mack MacDiarmid other than he was wealthy and had a reputation as a love-them-and-leave-them playboy.

She had done her own research and found a couple of articles about Mack online. Named after his father Robert but going by the nickname of Mack, he was a successful businessman and entrepreneur who had made millions in various property developments both in the UK and abroad. Crannochbrae was his ancestral home and he had restored it, managed and developed it since his father's death when he was a teenager. But the photos of him in the articles hadn't prepared her for seeing him in the flesh, even if it was from three storeys above. Tall and lean with a rangy build, Mack MacDiarmid had an aura of command and authority that was unmistakable...and a little unnerving to say the least. Would he see through her act? Why had she thought she could pull this off? She wasn't used to being around men like Mack MacDiarmid. Powerful, dynamic men who had made their fortune from being whip smart and intuitive.

As Fraser MacDiarmid's older brother, Mack was part of the wedding party, which meant there would be no way of avoiding coming into contact with him. Although, since she would only be in her sister's shoes for the rehearsal, the contact would hopefully be limited. But had Mack ever met her twin before?

Elspeth grabbed her phone off the bed where she'd left it earlier, and, pointedly ignoring the ten text messages and five missed calls from her mother, quickly fired off a text to her twin.

Have you ever met Mack MacDiarmid in person?

The three little dots appeared to signal Elodie was texting back. And then the message came through.

No.

What about Fraser, the groom?

The phone indicated her message had been read but there was no answer, which either meant Elodie was called away to her important meeting or didn't want to answer. Elspeth had a feeling it was the latter. She smoothed a hand down over her churning stomach. Why had she agreed to do this? She took a calming breath and pushed away from the wall. She agreed to do this because she wanted her sister to succeed in her new venture. Elodie was tired of modelling and wanted to express her creativity. It was up to Elspeth to pull this off for the next twenty-four hours. She knew her twin almost as well as she knew herself. She stared at her twin's face every day in the mirror. It was simply a matter of putting on her twin's make-up and clothes and adopting her twin's friendly and chatty, outgoing and super-confident personality and no one would be the wiser.

How hard could it be?

# CHAPTER TWO

ELSPETH MADE HER way down to one of the main reception rooms in the castle, where the bridal party was gathered for welcome drinks. In spite of her you-can-do-this pep talk earlier, a colony of razor-winged butterflies was attacking the lining of her stomach. She was dressed in one of her twin's designer outfits—an electric-blue satin sheath of a dress that clung to her body like a long, silky evening glove. The blue made her eyes pop, so too did the smoky make-up she had put on. The dress was way more revealing than any she would normally wear, but, hey, Cinderella had to get used to wearing a sparkly ball gown and glass slippers, right? Her twin's shoes weren't made of glass but they were higher than any Elspeth had ever worn before. And they cost more than a month's wages. She'd had to practise wearing them by doing laps of her bedroom before she ventured downstairs. She had only stumbled once, so she was quite pleased with herself.

Years of watching Elodie get ready for a photo shoot had certainly paid off. Elspeth's skin was flawless, her eyes highlighted by eyeshadow and eyeliner and lash-lengthening mascara. Her lips were shiny with strawberry-flavoured lip gloss and her pulse points sprayed with a heady musky perfume that had only made her sneeze once. So far.

But, make-up and beautiful clothes notwithstanding, Elspeth knew she was walking a fine line and, at any moment, one misstep could blow her cover. How on earth did undercover agents do this sort of thing day in and day out? It was enough to give you a stomach ulcer.

Elspeth was still a little wide-eyed about spending the weekend in an actual castle. How many people outside royalty owned their very own castle? But that was the sort of wealth Mack MacDiarmid possessed. His ancestry went back centuries and she couldn't help feeling a little impressed by her surroundings. There were so many rooms, so many stairs, so many turrets it was as if she had stepped inside a fairy tale. The grounds were extensive with both formal and wild gardens, rolling fields and dense woods backdropped by the craggy Highlands. Situated on the shore of a small loch, the estate was picturesque and private, the perfect setting for a wedding. Everything was in tip-top shape. No crumbling walls or sagging ceilings, no draughty corridors with inadequate lighting or heating, no dust sheets draped over furniture or cobwebs hanging from the cornices or the crystal chandeliers. There was even a shiny suit of armour in the gallery, along with huge portraits of previous generations of MacDiarmids. Huge whimsical flower arrangements adorned every room, her own room included. Only the wedding party was staying at the castle but, since she was one of six bridesmaids, she hoped she would be lost in the crowd.

But as soon as she walked into the reception room, Sabine, the bride, rushed over to her.

'Elodie! You look amazing as always.' Sabine did the air-kiss thing and stood back to run her gaze over Elspeth's outfit…well, her twin's outfit, that was. 'That blue is so stunning on you. And your make-up is so professional and we haven't even had the make-up artist, Maggie, do her magic on you yet.'

'Oh, this old thing?' Elspeth waved a hand in front of her twin's outfit in exactly the same dismissive manner Elodie would have used. 'You look lovely too. I'm sure you'll be the most gorgeous bride ever.' Okay, well, maybe her twin wouldn't have laid on the compliments quite so enthusiastically but Elspeth thought Sabine was a very pretty girl-next-door type who was positively glowing with happiness. It made her wonder if falling in love with the man of her dreams could work the same magic on her. As if. Who was going to fall in love with a girl who couldn't walk past a bowl of nuts without having a panic attack?

'I'm so honoured you could find time in your busy schedule to be my bridesmaid,' Sabine said. 'It means the world to me. You're such a fantastic role model at how to look fabulous without even trying.'

*Without even trying?* Elspeth had to hold back a spluttering laugh. She had been trying to turn herself into a glamour queen for the last two hours. Sheesh. How did her twin do this every day? It was positively exhausting.

'It's a privilege to be here,' Elspeth said with a smile. 'It's such a beautiful place to hold a wedding.'

'I know, right? Mack, Fraser's brother, was so generous to let us use it,' Sabine said. 'Have you had something to eat?' She beckoned over a waiter who was carrying an array of delicious-looking finger food on a silver tray. 'These are scrumptious. I've had three of them already.'

Elspeth studied the tray of food for a brief moment, deciding against taking anything off it. She had two EpiPens in her clutch purse but the last thing she wanted to do was blow her cover in the first hour by triggering her allergy. She had considered quietly alerting the catering staff to her dietary issue but decided against it. It would draw far more attention to herself than she wanted, especially as there was no record of her twin ever having an allergy. Who knew if a paparazzo was lurking about ready to leak something to the press? It was easier to avoid eating. Besides, she had fresh fruit and nut-free cookies in her suitcase. There was a lot she would do for her twin but starving herself was not one of them. 'Thank you but I'm not hungry.'

'No wonder you're so slim,' Sabine said with a rueful grimace. 'I could never be as disciplined as you are. I love my food too much.' She looked past Elspeth's shoulder and smiled a broad smile. 'Let me introduce you to your host and bridal-party partner for the weekend.' She took Elspeth by the arm and led her to the other side of the room.

'Mack, this is Elodie Campbell, the famous lingerie model I was telling you about.'

Mack MacDiarmid turned around and met her gaze for the second time that day. A frisson passed over her flesh, her heart rate sped up and her mouth went dry. He was taller than she had calculated—at least six foot four—with broad shoulders and piercing grey-blue eyes framed by prominent eyebrows. His hair was dark brown with one or two threads of silver at the temples giving him a distinguished, old-before-his-years aura. His hair was slightly wavy and casually styled with one or two curls kinked over his forehead, lending him a rakish look that made her heart flutter. His square jaw hadn't seen a razor in a day or two, which should have made him look unkempt but somehow did the opposite. The designer stubble was rich and dark with a light sprinkling of silver throughout that, if anything, made him even more heart-stoppingly attractive.

'How do you do?' Mack held out his hand and she slipped hers into its firm clasp. If his Scottish accent and whisky-rough voice weren't enough to dazzle her senses, his touch more than completed the job. His skin was dry and warm, his fingers long and tanned, and a zap of electricity shot from his hand to hers with lightning-fast speed.

'Pleased to meet you.' Elspeth couldn't get her voice above more than a scratchy whisper and was aware of scorching heat pooling in her cheeks. Eek. Her twin hadn't blushed since she was twelve. How convincing was she going to be if her cheeks fired up every time Mack MacDiarmid glanced her way?

Mack released her hand but his gaze remained tethered to hers with an unnerving intensity. 'Welcome to Crannochbrae.'

'Thank you. It's been ages since I've been to Scotland. It's such a beautiful place, especially here in the Highlands. You have a gorgeous home. The gardens are spectacular. You must have millions of bees in total raptures with all those flowers.' She knew she was talking too much but something about Mack's commanding presence and unwavering gaze deeply unsettled her. She got the sense he was not easily fooled, not easily deceived, not easily manipulated. She started to question her sanity in agreeing to switch places with her twin. Why had she thought she could do this convincingly? It had been easy to fool their father all those years ago—he had never been able to tell them apart even when they were babies and toddlers, even before he left their mother for another woman when they were five.

But Elspeth got the feeling Mack MacDiarmid was a man who never let anything escape his notice. Every little detail was noted, documented, filed away for reference, for clarification. For close investigative study.

Mack's gaze narrowed ever so slightly. 'Didn't you have a photo shoot on the island of Skye a couple of months ago?'

'I—I did?' Elspeth looked at him blankly for a moment, her heart skipping a beat. 'Oh, yes, I forgot about that, silly me. I do so much travelling I can't remember where I've been or how long ago it was. Yes, of course, Skye was stunningly beautiful.' Double eek. This was proving to be harder than she had first thought. Her twin was always dashing off to yet another shoot in an exotic location, so it was hard to keep up with her movements. Elspeth vaguely remembered Elodie mentioning something about freezing to death on a Scottish beach modelling next summer's swimwear range. She tucked a strand of hair back behind her ear and beamed up at him as her twin would have done.

Mack's smile didn't make the full distance to his penetrating eyes. 'You enjoy travelling for work?'

'Love it. So many places to see, so many people to meet. Of course, it's not always glamourous. There's a lot of waiting around on shoots, a lot of time in hair and make-up and living out of a suitcase and so on.' Elspeth was repeating all the things her twin had told her over the years but even to her own ears, it sounded inauthentic. As if she was playing a part, which she was. Would he see through it? He didn't seem the type of man to be easily taken in. He was too suave and sophisticated and street smart. Never had she felt more out of her depth. Like a teensy-weensy goldfish flung out of her tiny bowl into a vast ocean of whale sharks.

'Can I get you something to drink? A cocktail? Champagne? G and T? Wine?' Mack asked.

Unlike her twin, Elspeth rarely drank alcohol. She had never really developed a taste for it because she so rarely socialised. But she figured it would look odd if she didn't have what her sister would normally have. Besides, a little Dutch courage might come in handy right now. 'Champagne would be lovely, thank you.'

Mack moved away to fetch a drink for her and Elspeth took a moment to try and calm her racing pulse. She couldn't stop following Mack with her gaze, drawn to him in a way she couldn't explain. He was so...so dynamic. So potently, breath-snatchingly attractive. It was as if every other man she had ever met paled in comparison. Not that she had met a lot of men in a dating sense. After her last date when she was eighteen, she had ended up in hospital with anaphylactic shock. Her mother had almost had a breakdown over it and Elspeth hadn't dated since. But that was why she had moved out of home a month ago, so she could live without her mother hovering and fussing over her as if she were still a child. She wasn't a child. She was a fully grown adult and could take care of herself. And this weekend was a good chance to prove it, to herself if not her mother.

'So you've finally met my big brother,' a male voice said in an undertone from close behind her.

Elspeth turned and encountered Fraser MacDiarmid. She recognised him from the photo Elodie had shown her. He was good-looking but not in the same category as his older brother. He was an inch or two shorter and carried a bit more weight around his middle. His jaw wasn't as strong, his gaze not as direct, his aura not as dynamic. Fraser was bland and boring where his brother, Mack, was compelling and captivating.

'Oh, hello…' Elspeth was at a loss to know what else to say. She couldn't remember if her twin had met Fraser or not and mentally rewound her conversation and text messages with her. Surely it was just the bride Elodie knew? But there was a familiarity about Fraser's manner towards her—the way he was standing so close, for instance—that suggested he considered her twin far more than a passing acquaintance.

Fraser gave her a smile that wasn't really a smile. 'I know what you're up to, you know.' His voice was still pitched low, as if he didn't want others to overhear.

Elspeth straightened her shoulders and willed her knees not to tremble. 'I have no idea what you're talking about.' At least *that* wasn't a lie.

His smile became vicious, like a stray dog baring its teeth. A don't-mess-with-me-I'm-dangerous-if-provoked warning. He leaned a little closer, his beer-scented breath wafting over her face. 'You think you're so clever wangling an invitation to my wedding just to watch me squirm.'

Why would he feel the need to squirm? What exactly had gone on between Fraser

MacDiarmid and her twin? A fling? An affair? Elodie hadn't mentioned anything about a fling with the groom. She had casually dated on and off in the seven years since jilting her fiancé, Lincoln Lancaster, but never for longer than a week or two. She claimed she didn't want to be tied down. She insisted she wasn't looking for Mr Right and the white picket fence and a pram parked in the hallway. But something clearly had gone on between Fraser and Elodie. But what?

'I was flattered to be invited to be one of Sabine's bridesmaids,' Elspeth said, desperately trying to stay as cool and collected as her twin would have done.

'I bet you were.' Fraser raked her with his gaze. 'But if you so much as whisper one word of what happened between us that night in London, I'll deny everything and make you look like the troublemaking fool you are.'

Her heart banged against her ribcage and a cold shiver scuttled down her back. *What had happened between them?* As much as it shocked her to be threatened by a man who was clearly a bit of a bully, Elspeth stayed in her twin's character with renewed vigour, even with a little more confidence. After all, Fraser MacDiarmid clearly didn't suspect she was a stand-in—he was treating her as if she were indeed her twin. Someone with whom he had had some sort of encounter that he was now desperate to keep secret on the eve of his wedding.

Elspeth inched up her chin, her gaze pointed. 'But will your fiancée believe you?' She was proud of how sassy and defiant she sounded. So like Elodie it was kind of spooky. Not that she could ever be as confident and in charge as her twin, more was the pity. But it sure was rather thrilling to pretend.

But then she noticed Mack coming back with her glass of champagne, his intelligent gaze taking in the tense little tableau between her and his brother.

'Ooh, lovely,' Elspeth said, taking the glass off Mack with a smile bright enough to outshine the crystal chandeliers above. 'My favourite. Cheers.' She took a generous sip of the champagne and was pleasantly surprised to find she liked the taste. But maybe that was because it was the best champagne money could buy. No doubt Mack MacDiarmid would not serve cheap imported sparkling wine from the local off-licence at his brother's wedding. Or maybe it was because, right then, she needed all the help she could get to get through this ridiculous charade.

But *was* it so ridiculous?

The realisation drifted into her mind that, right now, a part of her was actually enjoying herself. She was a little out of her comfort zone, sure, but no one so far had guessed she wasn't Elodie, even Fraser, who apparently had had some sort of illicit tryst with her twin. *Go me*, she thought. Who knew she could act so convincingly? But—even more exciting—she was getting a buzz from being in the company of Mack MacDiarmid. Every time he came within a metre of her, every cell in her body tingled with awareness.

'Excuse me, I have to mingle with the other guests,' Fraser said, and strode away with a deep frown carved between his eyes.

Mack looked down at her with an unreadable expression on his face. 'Everything all right?'

Elspeth blinked up at him guilelessly. 'Sure. I'm having a marvellous time. Just super. Everything is just wonderful.'

His gaze drifted to her mouth, lingered there for a pulse-racing moment. 'Liar.' His voice was deep and rumbly and it did strange things to the base of her spine, making it all tingly and loose.

Elspeth had to remind herself she was pretending to be her twin. Elodie would not stand there with her heart pounding and her senses on high alert. She would not be intimidated by the most handsome man she had ever met. She would stand her ground and give as good as she got. 'You don't look like you're having a wonderful time either.'

'What makes you say that?'

She gave her version of one of her twin's classic insouciant one-shoulder shrugs. 'All these people you don't know or even particularly like traipsing all over your home all weekend, getting drunk and up to who knows what else.'

One side of his mouth tipped up in a cynical half-smile. 'Is that your plan? To get drunk and get up to who knows what else?'

Elspeth took another sip of her champagne, deciding it was as addictive as verbal sparring with the Laird of Crannochbrae. His eyes continued to hold hers in a challenging lock, his mouth still tilted in an enigmatic smile. 'I don't have a plan. I like to live moment to moment. It's way more fun.' She beamed another smile at him. 'You should try it some time, Mr Control Freak.' She drained her glass and set it down on a nearby table. *Mr Control Freak?* Eek. What had made her call him that? It sounded as though she was actually flirting with him.

She had never flirted with anyone. She had missed out on the flirting gene…or so she'd thought.

His eyes went back to her mouth and she had to fight the impulse to lick her lips. What was it about this man that made her feel so reckless and excited? Was it the champagne going to her head? Or was it Mack MacDiarmid's disturbingly attractive presence?

A flinty light came into his eyes. 'I would advise you, Miss Campbell, against doing anything that would jeopardise my brother's wedding this weekend. Do I make myself one hundred per cent crystal clear?' His tone was commanding, so commanding and dictatorial it made her bristle on her twin's behalf. What the hell did he think Elodie would do? Her twin might be a little wild at times but she would not wilfully sabotage someone's wedding day. She had sabotaged her own, sure, but that was another story. One Elodie had not yet told anyone the full details of, not even her. Elodie refused to talk about why she jilted her fiancé and Elspeth knew better than to keep pressing her to do so. Elodie could pout and stonewall for weeks on end if pushed too hard. She was so stubborn she could have made a career out of conducting training workshops for mules.

Elspeth moved a step closer to Mack, close enough to smell the citrus and woodsy notes of his aftershave. She had to fully extend her neck to maintain eye contact. Had to resist the sudden urge to stroke her hand down the peppery stubble on his lantern jaw to see if it felt as sexy as it looked. Had to stop herself from staring at his sensually contoured mouth and wondering what it would feel like against her own. 'You're not the boss of me but I bet you'd like to be.'

*Oh. My. God. Listen to me. I am so nailing impersonating Elodie right now.*

A line of tension rippled across his jaw and his gaze hardened another notch. 'You're way out of your league playing with me.'

Elspeth suspected even her outgoing don't-mess-with-me twin would be way out of her league playing with Mack, let alone her quiet and shy and socially inexperienced self. She lowered her gaze to the firm line of his mouth, her stomach bottoming out. 'What makes you think I want to play with you?'

He held her gaze for a long throbbing moment. 'I know your type.'

'And what type is that, pray tell?'

'The type of woman who likes to be the centre of attention.'

Elspeth lifted her eyebrows in an exaggerated manner. 'My, oh, my, what an appalling opinion you have of me—someone you've only just met. But don't worry, Mr MacDiarmid. It's not my intention to outshine the bride. This is her wedding weekend, not mine.'

'I heard about your ill-fated wedding day. Tell me—how did your fiancé feel about being left standing at the altar? Are you still on speaking terms?' There was a note of censure in his tone that, in all honesty, Elspeth had heard in her own voice when asking her twin about why she had done such a thing. That awful day was still etched in her mind. Seeing the look of bewilderment and then thunderous fury on Elodie's fiancé's face. The shocked embarrassment of the guests, the horror on their mother's face. Everyone turning to her and insisting she must have known something as Elodie's identical twin and why hadn't she let them know, blah blah blah. It had been beyond upsetting and embarrassing to admit she had known nothing. She had been just as blindsided as everyone else.

'It was seven years ago,' Elspeth said with a parody of her twin's nonchalance. 'He's forgotten all about me now.' That wasn't a lie either. Lincoln Lancaster had only ever had eyes for Elodie and would have probably forgotten the existence of her shy twin after all this time. And hopefully everyone else at the wedding that day. But whether Lincoln had forgotten Elodie was another matter.

'How well do you know Sabine?'

'Clearly well enough for her to want me to be one of her bridesmaids.' Elspeth gave him another plastic smile straight out of the party girl's playbook.

'And my brother, Fraser?'

Elspeth was aware of heat pooling in her cheeks and her smile fell away. 'Wh-what about him?' Her voice didn't sound as steady as she would have liked. And nor was her heart rate.

Mack's eyes became diamond hard. 'Describe your relationship with him.'

Elspeth pinched her lips together and held his gaze with a defiant glare. 'What are you implying?'

He gave a low deep grunt of cynical laughter that made her bristle from head to foot. 'You know exactly what I'm talking about.'

If only she did know. Elspeth was furious with her twin for putting her in such a compromising situation without giving her the full picture. How was she supposed to do a convincing job of pretending to be her twin when she didn't know what her twin had been up to? 'I hardly think it is any business of yours, Mr MacDiarmid.' Her voice was so tart it could have done a lemon out of a job.

Mack stepped a little closer and her breath caught in her throat and her cheeks heated up another notch. But it wasn't just her cheeks that were hot—her whole body was on fire, as if he had triggered an inferno in her flesh. 'I'm making it my business.' His tone had a gravelly edge that sent tingles down her spine, so too did the smoky grey-blue of his eyes.

'If you're so keen on finding out, why don't you ask your brother?'

'I'm asking you.'

'I refuse to discuss this while there are people about.' Elspeth began to move away before she got too far in over her head but one of his hands captured her slim wrist on the way past. She stopped dead, not because his grip was forceful—it wasn't. But because his touch was electrifying and it sent tingling shock waves through her entire body.

Elspeth looked down at his long, tanned fingers curled around her wrist, her heart slipping from its moorings in her chest. She hadn't been touched by a man in a decade. His touch set fire to her skin, every whorl of his fingers searing her flesh like a scorching brand. She brought her gaze back up to his and injected icy disdain in her voice. 'If you're so keen to avoid making a scene at your brother's wedding rehearsal, I suggest you take your hand off me this instant.'

The air was charged with a strange energy like a tight invisible wire stretching, stretching, stretching almost to snapping point.

Elspeth held his gaze with a strength of willpower she hadn't known she possessed. She would *not* be intimidated by him. She would not scuttle away like a scared little rabbit in front of a big bad wolf. She would stand up to him and enjoy every heart-stopping moment. Never had she felt so exhilarated, so alive and aware of her body. Flickers of lust stirred between her thighs, her breasts tingled and tightened, her blood rocketed through her veins at breakneck speed.

But as exciting as it was to stand up to Mack MacDiarmid, she couldn't quite forget she was playing a role. She was *pretending* to be Elodie. And as empowering as it felt to interact with such a dashingly handsome man, she had to remember it was a charade. She could never be part of the world her twin lived in. She could do a walk-on part for twenty-four hours but that was all. It was crazy to think otherwise.

Mack's fingers loosened a fraction but only enough to reposition so his thumb could measure her racing-off-the-charts pulse. 'Why do you I make you so nervous?' His tone was silky, his gaze penetrating.

Elspeth hoisted her chin. 'I'm not intimidated by you.' Or at least, she was pretending she wasn't intimidated. Pretending she wasn't rattled, unnerved, intrigued and bewitched by him.

He gave an indolent smile and stroked his thumb across her blue-veined wrist, her sensitive skin tingling, fizzing in delight. 'Meet me in the library in half an hour. We'll continue our discussion in private.' He released her wrist and turned and walked away before she could think of an answer. Or a reason not to meet him.

Elspeth let out a long wobbly breath like someone squeezing the last bit of air out of a set of bagpipes. Meet him in private? To discuss what? Things she had absolutely no clue about? Being anywhere alone with Mack MacDiarmid was asking for trouble. He only had to look at her to send her heart racing and her blood pumping. She looked down at her wrist where his fingers had touched her and a frisson passed through her body. Her skin felt as if it had been permanently branded—it was still tingling, all the nerves rioting beneath her skin.

At least her twin would be here first thing in the morning, so she could get out of this farce before she made a complete and utter fool of herself. If only Elodie had prepared her a little more. Why hadn't her twin told her what had occurred between her and Mack's younger brother, Fraser? For something had gone on, of that she was sure. She picked up another glass of champagne off a passing waiter and took a sip to moisten her powder-dry mouth. The last hour had given her a taste for top-shelf French champagne and a brooding Scotsman.

And she didn't know which one would do the most damage—the demon drink or the devilishly handsome Mack MacDiarmid.

Mack cornered his brother a short time later in what used to be the music room. It was now a spare sitting room but it wasn't used that often. He had sold his beloved piano years ago and had never got around to replacing it. He had given up his dreams of a musical career and concentrated on salvaging the family's estate instead. Mack closed the door with a resounding click and eyeballed his brother. 'Tell me what's going on between you and Elodie Campbell.'

Fraser's gaze darted away from his as he walked to the other side of the room to pick up an ornament off a side table. 'Nothing's going on.' He put the ornament down again and then straightened a photo of their mother.

'But something did go on between you.' Mack framed it as a statement because he knew when his brother was lying. 'I thought you were worried Elodie Campbell might dance on the tables or drink too much and act a little inappropriately with the father of the bride or something. But *this*?'

Fraser loosened his tie with one hand as if it were choking him. Beads of perspiration dotted his forehead. 'It was nothing.' He clenched his fists and added with greater emphasis, 'It meant nothing. *She* meant nothing.'

Mack drew in a breath and slowly released it. 'I'm the last person to judge someone for having a one-night stand but were you engaged to Sabine at the time?'

His brother's cheeks developed twin flags of colour high on his cheekbones. 'I'm not going to answer that because it's none of your damn business.'

Mack frowned. 'Because it's too confronting to openly admit you've been a prize jerk?'

Fraser gave him a glowering look. 'It was only the once. No damage has been done. Sabine doesn't know and I'd like it to stay that way.'

Mack let out a curse in Gaelic. 'Damage *has* been done. Sabine thinks the man she's marrying tomorrow is loyal and faithful. How many other women have you been with since you've been engaged to her?'

'It's none of your business, Mack. You're not my father.'

'No, but you're turning into ours,' Mack shot back. 'Dad didn't have the guts to be honest about the mistakes he made, the lies he told, the truths about himself he refused to face either. He was a coward and it destroyed our mother's life and that of his lover and child. Do you really want to do that to Sabine? Because that's the way it starts—one lie, one misstep, one betrayal and then a thousand lies and cover-ups until it all comes crumbling down around you like a house of cards.'

Fraser gave a convulsive swallow, his eyes showing raw fear. 'I can't tell Sabine. It'll destroy her. She thinks I've never met Elodie before. She met her at a charity function and got a little star-struck by her. Next thing I know they're chatting online and, hey presto, she's invited her to be one of the bloody bridesmaids. I'm sure Elodie engineered it just to make trouble. I couldn't say I didn't want her in the wedding party because Sabine would have wondered why.' He turned away and scraped his hand through his hair. 'Can you imagine the scandal it will cause if it comes out now? What the press will make of it?'

'Why did you do it? Aren't you happy with Sabine?'

Fraser threw him a worldly glance. 'You've met Elodie. Why do you think I did it?'

Mack had no argument with his brother on finding Elodie Campbell stunningly beautiful. Any man with his fair share of testosterone would find her attractive. But there was something about her that didn't add up and he was determined to find out exactly what it was. It was as if she was acting a part, playing a role of femme fatale that didn't sit all that comfortably with her. He was prepared to accede that most public figures had another side to their personality, especially if they were representing a brand. They could be quite different in their private lives away from the spotlight. He was convinced the young woman he caught a glimpse of from the upstairs window was not the same woman who sparred with him a few minutes ago. It wasn't just about the hair and make-up and fancy clothes. Something about El-odie Campbell puzzled him and he would not rest until he figured her out. 'Just be-cause you find a woman attractive doesn't mean you're entitled to sleep with her. Did she know you were in a committed relation-ship at the time?'

The dull flush on his brother's cheekbones darkened. 'No.'

'So you lied to her too.'

Fraser rolled his eyes and spun on his heels again. 'She would have slept with me any-way. She's a slut. Everyone knows that.'

Mack ground his teeth so hard he thought his molars would crack like his grandmoth-er's heirloom porcelain china. How had his younger brother become such a misogynist? 'Careful, your double standard is showing. A slut is basically a woman living by a man's morals, so I would advise you not to use such an offensive term.'

'You would *advise*.' Fraser leaned on the word and made a scoffing noise in the back of his throat. 'It's all you ever do—tell me what I should or shouldn't do.'

Mack had had to step into a father role from the age of sixteen when their father committed suicide after his double life and the massive debts he'd built up were suddenly exposed. It had devastated their mother and Fraser, but Mack had had to set aside his own shock and grief and take control before any more damage was done. But even so, Fraser had subsequently acted out throughout his teens, skipping school, failing subjects he used to be star pupil in, dabbling in drugs and excessive alcohol. It had been a nightmare for Mack trying to keep his family together, to maintain some sense of normality when everything had been turned upside down. He'd had to put an end to his own career aspirations in order to run the estate.

Music had been his passion, his love, his everything and he'd had to give it up. He hadn't touched a piano since. It was as if a part of him had died along with his father. He'd had to work three jobs, sell off valuable heirloom items he wished he hadn't had to sell, beg and borrow huge amounts of money to cover the hair-raising debts his father had left behind. It had taken years of hard work and sacrifice to get the estate back in the black. 'Only because you seem incapable of getting your act together. I know it was rough on you when Dad died. It was rough on all of us, Mum in particular. But you're not fourteen any more, Fraser. You're a grown man about to get married. You owe it to Sabine to be straight with her.'

'It'll hurt her…'

Mack gave him a look. 'A pity you didn't think of that when you unzipped your—'

'Elodie started it. She came on to me.'

'And you had no choice? No moral compass to guide you? You just got down and dirty and forgot about everything but getting it off with a beautiful woman behind your fiancée's back.'

'You're such a hypocrite.' Fraser curled his lip. 'You've slept with dozens of women.'

'I'm not denying it, but I have never done so while in love with someone else.' Mack had never been in love. Had in fact avoided any emotional entanglements that would require him to invest in a relationship longer than a week or two. He wondered if he was even capable of loving someone in that way. Love was supposed to be blind and in their mother's case it certainly had been. But when it came to that, he too had been blind about his father. Blindly devoted to his dad without realising his father was living a double life. Racking up gambling debts, keeping a mistress and child in another city for years, spending money he didn't have to fund his crazy lifestyle. In hindsight, Mack could recall each of his father's blatant lies. Lies that still hurt to this day. The fact that his dad had tricked him into thinking he was working hard for them for weeks at a time, missing important dates—birthdays, parent-teacher meetings, key sporting events—when the truth was he was with his other family.

The betrayal of trust had been life-changing for Mack. He no longer chose to be blind to a person's faults. He no longer possessed a pair of rose-coloured glasses. He went into relationships with his eyes wide open and got out of them before any damage was done. Trusting someone, loving someone made you blind to their faults, to their lies, to their cover-ups. He kept emotion out of his relationships. They were transactional and temporary and could be terminated without tears.

Fraser's expression was belligerent. 'I'm not going to sabotage my own wedding by confessing one little mistake to Sabine. And I'd appreciate it if you would keep Elodie Campbell under control as I asked you to.'

Mack had a feeling trying to control Elodie Campbell even for twenty-four seconds was going to be a challenge. But, hey, he liked a challenge and she was a rather beautiful and intriguing one.

But controlling his own red-hot attraction to her was going to be the kicker.

# CHAPTER THREE

ELSPETH WENT BACK to her room upstairs to phone Elodie without anyone listening in. It was no surprise to see another raft of text messages from her mother. She blew out a breath and quickly pinged off a text assuring her mother that she was fine and having a wonderful time. What was one more lie when she had told heaps so far? She then called her twin's number.

'What the hell happened between you and Fraser MacDiarmid?' she asked as soon as Elodie answered.

'Nothing.'

'It can't have been nothing. I just had him snarling in my ear downstairs, warning me to keep my mouth shut. I don't even know what it is I'm supposed to be keeping quiet about. The least you could have done is tell me. I feel like I'm on stage in a play in the

West End, playing to a full house after mem-orising the wrong script.'

Elodie let out a sigh heavy enough to send a helicopter into a tailspin. 'I didn't tell you because I'm embarrassed about it.' She paused for a beat and continued, 'I had a one-night stand with him. I'm not even at-tracted to him but I'd just run into Lincoln and his latest squeeze in the same London bar… I don't know…it made me a little crazy. I got chatting to Fraser and then I went back to his room. End of story.'

Elspeth knew her twin was a little reck-less at times but picking up strangers in a bar was completely out of character. Yes, she was flirtatious and daring and outgoing but, as far as Elspeth knew, her sister wasn't a one-night-stand-with-a-stranger type of girl. But did she really know her twin as well as she thought? Elodie had always claimed she hadn't been in love with Lincoln Lancaster. That their whirlwind courtship had been out of balance from the start, for he'd been the one to insist on getting married when they had only known each other a couple of months. Why, then, would running into him with his latest lover upset Elodie so much?

'The least you could have done is tell me. I'm in over my head and I—'

'If I'd told you, you wouldn't have agreed to switch places,' Elodie said.

'Given the circumstances, why did you accept the role of bridesmaid in the first place? You said Sabine was only a passing acquaintance. You could have politely declined and—'

'I accepted before I realised who she was engaged to. Once I found out, it was too late to come up with an excuse not to accept the invitation. Besides, I figured it was a way to pay back Fraser for being such a sleaze.'

Elspeth suppressed a cold shudder. 'The sex between you was…consensual, wasn't it?'

'Yes, but he was a selfish lover and he didn't tell me he was engaged at the time. I would never have gone back to his room if I'd known that. I wanted to teach him a lesson and his delightfully friendly fiancée gave me the perfect way to do it.'

'But what about Sabine? Did you consider her in your plan for revenge?'

There was a weighted silence.

'Not at the time but since, yes.'

'Is that why you sent me instead of coming yourself? Your conscience got the better of you?' Elspeth asked.

'Partly, I guess, but I really did have a meeting here in London. I've only just finished it.'

'How did it go?'

'They want me to meet with them again tomorrow to discuss it further.'

A stone slab landed on the floor of Elspeth's stomach. *'Tomorrow?* But you're meant to be here first thing in the morning to switch places with me. In fact, shouldn't you be getting on a flight right now as you promised?'

'I can't be there. You'll have to keep up the act. It's only for another twenty-four hours. You've got this far without anyone guessing. Just keep doing what you're doing and everything will be sweet. Look—I've got to dash. I'm supposed to be meeting up with everyone from the meeting for drinks. Bye.'

Elspeth stared at the dead phone in her hand, her heart sinking in despair. Eek! Another twenty-four hours wearing her party-girl twin's shoes.

But what if she fell flat on her face?

Mack wondered if he needed his head examined for organising a private meeting with

Elodie Campbell in the library. But the temptation to squirrel her away from the rest of the wedding party was too irresistible. Besides wanting to hear her side of her fling with his younger brother, he had a burning desire to understand more about her character. She was warm and friendly towards Sabine, acting as if butter wouldn't melt in her mouth, and yet, if it was true she'd slept with Fraser, what sort of friend of the bride did that make her? Fraser had admitted Elodie hadn't known he was engaged at the time of their brief encounter, but, still, agreeing to be Sabine's bridesmaid seemed a little inappropriate under the circumstances. What exactly was motivating Elodie to be here? She had a busy schedule taking her all over the world—it would have been easy enough to politely decline the invitation. And Sabine, being a sweet and generous-natured young woman, would have understood.

No, there was more to Elodie Campbell than he'd first thought. She was feisty and spirited when interacting with him and yet, every now and again he caught her chewing at her lower lip, looking uncertain and way out of her depth. And what about those blushes? He hadn't thought someone with the party-girl reputation Elodie had would blush so readily or so deeply. Or was that because she felt guilty about her fling with the groom of her friend?

But there was another reason Mack wanted time alone with her. He wanted to make sure she had no ulterior motive for being at his brother's wedding. Sabine had been a wonderful influence on Fraser over the last year or so and Mack was determined their wedding would go ahead. It had to. Apart from the money he had spent on the young couple's nuptials, Mack was worried that Fraser might spin out of control if Sabine called it quits. Sabine's wealthy businessman father had promoted Fraser high up in his company and given him extra privileges that would be taken away in a heartbeat if anything went awry with his beloved only daughter. Mack didn't want to think about Fraser losing his job, the career pathway that had been so stabilising for him.

Mack had to keep Elodie Campbell under control. He had to make sure the wedding went ahead without any dramas.

And one way to do that was to keep Elodie's attention focussed on himself instead of his brother.

And that, he decided, would be nothing if not entertaining.

* * *

Elspeth considered ignoring Mack's command to meet him in the library but curiosity got the better of her. And not just because the library of a centuries-old castle was to her one of the most exciting places in the world to visit. The enigmatic Mack MacDiarmid was even more exciting.

Dangerously so.

Elspeth found the library and was pleased he wasn't yet there. It gave her time to peruse the floor-to-ceiling shelves, to drool over some of the titles housed there. It was an archivist's dream to be surrounded by priceless editions that were hundreds of years old. There were journals and diaries from some of Mack's ancestors and she wished she had more time so she could read through them all. The room had a velvet-covered wing chair and a sofa in front of the windows that overlooked the dense woods behind the castle. A tall standard lamp was situated beside the wing chair, providing a perfect reading place, and she pictured herself curled up in it with one of the ancient books, with Highland snow falling softly and silently outside. She placed her clutch purse on one of the shelves and began to examine some of the titles. Her eyes nearly popped out of her head at some of the treasures housed on the shelves. Did Mack know the value of these books? Had they been archived and insured? She stared at row after row of priceless titles, her breath catching in wonder, her hands itching to examine them. But books as old as these needed special care. Cotton gloves for handling and a controlled-temperature environment to preserve them for generations to come.

The sound of the door clicking shut behind her made Elspeth spin round from the bookshelves. 'You have a lot of wonderful books. I can't believe what a treasure trove you've got here. Have they ever been valued or archived? Are they adequately insured?'

Mack stepped further into the room, his expression difficult to read. 'The most valuable were sold a few years ago.'

'But there must be others here that are worth a mint.' She gazed back up at the shelves and pointed. 'That one there—the leather-bound one I'm sure is a rare edition of *The Canterbury Tales*. A copy of it sold for several million pounds a while back. Could you get it down for me? And do you have a pair of cotton gloves?'

Mack took so long to answer, Elspeth

turned round to look at him. 'Is something wrong?'

He stepped further into the light coming from the chandelier above. 'You have an interest in rare books?' His expression was still largely inscrutable but a piercing light in his gaze sent a tingling shiver skittering across her scalp.

Elspeth suddenly realised her gaffe. Her twin was a lingerie model who had chosen to leave school before she got her GCSEs in her quest to make a career out of modelling. There were numerous interviews Elodie had given about her struggle with dyslexia and how she had spent most of her childhood avoiding reading. 'Erm…yes, it's kind of a hobby of mine…' She turned away and gnawed at her lip, her heart racing so hard and fast she thought she might faint. She could feel her cheeks heating…so much for the controlled-temperature environment. At this rate, her cheeks would turn the precious books into ashes within minutes.

'What other hobbies do you have?'

Elspeth forced herself to face him again, painting a smile on her face, while her heart did somersaults in her chest. 'I draw. I dabble in watercolours.' At least those things were true. It was a talent she and her twin shared.

Mack came up to where she was standing, his eyes holding hers in an unwavering lock. 'Tell me something. Why did you accept the invitation to be Sabine's bridesmaid?'

The question blindsided her for a moment. She moistened her lips and averted her gaze, focussing it on the collar of his shirt. 'I like Sabine. She's a sweetheart.' That was also true, Elspeth decided. Sabine was a warm and friendly soul who deserved better than Mack's cheating younger brother, Fraser. She wished she could warn Sabine about the man she was marrying tomorrow but how could she do it without blowing her cover? Sabine would be hurt by not one but three betrayals—her fiancé's cheating, Elodie being the person he cheated with and Elspeth standing in for her twin as bridesmaid.

'Then why did you sleep with her fiancé, my younger brother?'

Elspeth swallowed. 'I—I don't wish to discuss—'

'We are not leaving this room until we have discussed it.' His tone had that determined edge that had so irritated her before.

Elspeth gave him a frosty look. 'You can hardly hold me prisoner.'

His grey-blue eyes darkened to gunmetal-grey. 'Don't tempt me.'

The air crackled with tension. A throbbing tension Elspeth could feel in her body. The low and deep secret tug of desire, the heightening of her senses, the flaring of her nostrils, the lowering of her lashes, the soft parting of her lips.

Mack's gaze became hooded and dipped to her mouth and lingered there for a heart-stopping moment. The tension in the air tightened another notch as if all the oxygen particles had been removed. Elspeth couldn't take her eyes off his lips, the sensual contour of them totally mesmerising. Was he going to kiss her? Her heart flip-flopped and she moistened her lips with a nervous dart of her tongue. She mustn't let herself get carried away but, oh, how amazing it would be to feel those firm lips against her own. She hadn't been kissed in a decade. She was a virgin who was nudging thirty with only one kiss under her belt.

One almost deadly kiss that had put her in hospital and sent her mother under the care of a therapist for over a year.

It was a timely reminder that Elspeth was way out of her depth. She might pretend to be sassy and in control but she was playing a role. She was shy and inexperienced Elspeth, not street-smart and ebullient Elodie.

Elspeth raised her chin a fraction. 'Right now, I'm tempted to slap your arrogant face.'

'Then maybe I should give you an even better reason to do so.' Mack took her by the upper arms in a gentle but firm hold, the erotic intent in his glittering gaze unmistakable.

'W-wait.' Elspeth placed her hands flat against his rock-hard chest. 'Have you been eating nuts?'

His brows came together in a deep frown. 'What?'

She licked her lips with another flick of her tongue. 'I can't allow you to kiss me if you've eaten nuts. I—I hate the taste. I find it nauseating.'

Mack measured her with his gaze for a long moment, his hands still on her upper arms. 'Do you want me to kiss you?'

*Gulp.* Elspeth blinked and she could feel scorching heat storming into her face. 'Erm… I—I thought *you* wanted to kiss me.'

His gaze dipped to her mouth for a nano-second before reconnecting with her gaze. 'Now, there's a thought,' he drawled, his lips tilting in a smile that made her legs go weak. 'But I'm not sure it would be wise under the circumstances.' His hands fell away from her arms but he didn't move away.

'Because of the...the nut thing?'

'Are you allergic to them or just don't like the taste?'

Elspeth found herself confessing the truth. 'Erm...allergic. Badly. I can't even touch the same surface where nuts have been or use products that have almond oil in them.'

'That's tough. It must be hard to avoid them.'

'I'm used to it. I—I don't like to make too big a thing of it. It's not good for my image, you know?'

'You haven't thought of being the poster girl for peanut allergies? Using your profile to campaign for much-needed funding in allergy research—that sort of thing?'

Elspeth's cheeks felt as if they were on fire. At this rate, she could solve an energy crisis for a small nation. 'I like to use my influence in other ways. I don't like being reminded of my faulty immune system.'

He studied her for a lengthy moment. 'All nuts or just peanuts?'

'All nuts but peanuts are the worst.'

'I'm not a fan of them either.'

Her eyes widened. 'You're not?'

'I once inhaled one when I was a toddler and had to be rushed to hospital. I haven't eaten them since.'

She couldn't stop staring at his mouth, the shape of it captivating her. 'Oh…wow, I've heard that's pretty dangerous for little kids…'

'It is.'

He was still so close to her she could feel the warm waft of his breath against her face. Could see the flecks of grey in the blue of his eyes, reminding her of smooth stones at the bottom of a riverbed. Could feel her body responding to his proximity with soft little flickers of awareness, flutters of lust and need that bloomed inside her like an exotic flower under the searing rays of the sun. He slid a hand along the side of her face, his touch so mesmerising, so thrilling she was totally spellbound, trapped in a sensual stasis. She thought of stepping back away from his light touch but that was as far as it went— a thought. Not one muscle in her body agreed with acting on it.

'So, given that we've established I haven't consumed nuts, what harm is one little kiss going to do, hmm?' he said in a low rumbly voice, his eyes drifting to her mouth once more.

Elspeth disguised another gulp, her own gaze drinking in every contour of his mouth. 'So, you *do* want to kiss me?' She hadn't meant to sound quite so gobsmacked. Her twin probably kissed men all the time without a single qualm.

Mack's hand moved further back along her face until it was embedded in her hair, sending a shivery wave of pleasure across her scalp. 'I find myself incredibly tempted to do so.'

Elspeth stared at his mouth with her pulse skyrocketing. 'But...but *why*?' Her tone had taken gobsmacked to a whole new level.

He gave a soft breath of a laugh. 'Because for some reason I find you irresistibly attractive.'

What he found attractive was her version of Elodie, Elspeth quickly reminded herself. It had nothing to do with *her*. A sharp twinge of disappointment got her under the ribs. Would someone as suave and sophisticated as Mack MacDiarmid want to kiss the real Elspeth? Not flipping likely. 'That's very flattering but—'

'There's nothing about you having a nut allergy in any of the interviews you've given. Why is that?' Mack's tone had a probing edge that sent a wave of alarm through her.

'Yes, well, I didn't want to make a big issue out of it...or to have someone sabotage me just before an important shoot. Believe me, it's a jungle out there.' Elspeth was pleased with how she was handling the situation. Who knew she could think on her feet so well? She had clearly missed her calling as an improvisation actor.

His frown deepened. 'Another model would actually do that?'

'Who knows? It's very competitive out there on the runway. I decided long ago not to risk it.' She forced another smile on her lips and added, 'Erm…shouldn't we be getting back to the rest of the party?'

'What's the hurry?' His hand slid deeper into the cloud of her hair, sending more tingles over her scalp and a shiver skittering down her spine.

She was conscious of his strongly muscled thighs standing within inches of her own. Conscious of the citrus and wood notes of his aftershave. Conscious of how much she wanted him to kiss her. Conscious of the way his gaze kept tracking to her mouth. Her lips tingled in anticipation. Every inch of her skin tightening and twitching with awareness. 'They might be wondering what we're up to…'

His lazy smile did strange things to her heart rate. 'Maybe they think I'm making mad passionate love to you in the library.'

'Wh-why would they think that? I only met you an hour or so ago.'

'That's not stopped you before, or so I'm told.'

She moved out of his hold, wrapping her arms around her middle, her face hot as fire. 'You shouldn't believe everything you're told.'

'I don't.' Something in his tone made her turn back to look at him. His expression was inscrutable except for that enigmatic smile curving his sensual lips.

'Why do I get the feeling you're playing with me like a cat does a mouse?'

Mack came back to stand in front of her. 'I'm fascinated by you.'

She disguised a nervous swallow. 'Wh-why?' She could safely say no one had ever been fascinated by her before.

He picked up a loose strand of her red-gold hair and wound it around his index finger. The slight tension on her scalp sent a delicious frisson through her body. The laser focus of his gaze sending her heart rate into the danger zone. But then, everything about Mack MacDiarmid spelled danger. She had never met a more potently attractive man. Never been so close to a man she could almost sense his body's primal reaction to her.

A primal reaction that triggered a firestorm in her own female flesh. 'You're a mystery I want to solve.'

'I can assure you there's nothing mysterious about me.' Why couldn't she get her voice above a throaty whisper? Why couldn't she just step away from him and get the hell out of the library before she lost all control of her senses? She was hypnotised by his alluring presence, drugged by his touch, addicted to the sound of his voice, hungry for the crush of his sensual lips on hers.

'Ah, but that's where I disagree,' he said, slowly unwinding her hair from his finger. 'As soon as I saw you at the upstairs window earlier today, I sensed you were hiding something.'

Elspeth rapid-blinked and flicked her hair back behind her shoulders. 'Of course I was hiding something. I was standing there in nothing but my wrap, for pity's sake.'

'You've been seen in much less by millions of people all over the world.'

She bit her lip for a nanosecond. 'Look— I really think we should get back to the rest of the bridal party. The rehearsal's about to start in a few minutes. It'll look odd if we're not there to play our role.'

'You're right.' Mack stepped back from

her with a mercurial smile. 'We have both been assigned an important role to play this weekend, yes?' There was a cryptic quality to his tone that made her heart rate spike once more.

'Erm, yes…' Elspeth gave a nervous swallow. 'We have.'

But her job this weekend would be a whole lot easier if Mack MacDiarmid weren't so sharply intelligent and eagle-eyed observant.

Or so deliciously, knee-wobblingly attractive.

'What are your feelings towards my brother?'

Elspeth decided to be brutally honest. 'I don't think he's good enough for Sabine.'

A knot of tension flickered in his jaw and a hard light came into his eyes. 'So, you'd like to see the wedding called off? Is that what you're saying?'

Elspeth forced herself to hold his diamond-hard gaze. 'Do you think he's truly in love with her?'

His mouth twisted in a cynical manner. 'I'm not sure my brother understands the meaning of true love.'

'Do you?' The question was out before she could monitor her tongue.

Mack gave a harsh grunt of a laugh. 'I understand it, I've seen it and the damage it can cause when it's unrequited, but I haven't experienced it myself.'

'Nor have I.'

'Not even with your ex-fiancé?'

Elspeth mentally kicked herself for momentarily slipping out of character. But had Elodie actually loved Lincoln Lancaster? Their relationship had been hotly passionate from the get-go and Elspeth had felt a little envious that no one had ever looked at her the smouldering way Lincoln had looked at her twin. Elodie had claimed to love him right up until the day of the wedding. Then, as if a switch had been flipped, she'd insisted it was all a mistake, that she was too young to settle down, that Lincoln wasn't the right person for her, etc, etc. It had shocked everyone, Elspeth most of all because she had truly thought Elodie had found her soulmate only to watch her throw him aside as if he were a toy she was no longer interested in. 'I decided I was too young to settle down. I thought it better to call off the wedding rather than go through a costly divorce further down the track.'

'But did you love him?' His gaze was laser-pointer direct.

Elspeth raised her chin at a combative height. 'My feelings towards Lincoln Lancaster are none of your business.' She spun away but before she could move a step, his hand came down on her wrist, his fingers curling around her slender bones in a gentle but firm hold.

'What about your feelings for my brother, Fraser? You cleverly avoided answering me before.'

Elspeth knew she should be brushing off his hand but, just for a moment, she let it stay exactly where it was. The warmth and tensile strength of his fingers on her wrist sent shivers racing up and down her spine and a spurt of liquid heat to her core. How could a man's touch be so magnetic? So intensely sensual? 'You want the honest truth?' she asked with a pointed look.

'If you can manage it, yes.' The cynical edge to his tone matched the glint in his eyes and both ramped up her ire.

Elspeth pulled her wrist out of his hold and rubbed at it as if it had been burned by his touch, which it had, come to think of it. A searing burn that travelled all the way to the core of her being, simmering there in secret. 'I dislike him intensely.'

'So you regret hooking up with him?'

Elspeth couldn't meet his gaze. 'Of course. It's put me in such an awkward position...'

Wasn't that the truth? She chewed at her lower lip and added, 'I hate the thought of Sabine finding out but, again, I hate the thought of her marrying him tomorrow without knowing he cheated on her.' She returned her gaze to his. 'He should have told her well before this, so she could decide whether she wanted to continue their relationship or not. She thinks she's marrying a devoted and loyal partner but instead she's marrying a cheat and a liar.' Elspeth knew she was hardly one to criticise someone for lying when all she had done so far this weekend was do exactly that—lie and deceive people.

'So you believe in honesty in intimate relationships?'

Elspeth's gaze skittered away from his. 'As far as possible.'

'Meaning?'

She glanced back at him but his expression was inscrutable. 'I'd like to think if I was in a committed relationship with someone they would honour me by being truthful about their feelings. If they felt, for instance, their needs weren't being met in some way, wouldn't it be better to talk about it rather than have those needs met clandestinely with someone else?'

'I couldn't agree more.'

There was a silence that was so intense Elspeth was sure she heard a rose petal drop from the flower arrangement on the antique table in front of the window.

Then the silence was broken by the click-clacking sound of approaching footsteps and before Elspeth could put some distance between her and Mack, Sabine came in with a wide smile. 'Oh, here you two are. What on earth are you up to in here?' Her eyes twinkled like a fairy godmother on a matchmaking mission.

'I'm so sorry,' Elspeth said, moving away from Mack, conscious of the fiery heat pooling in her cheeks. 'Are we holding up the rehearsal?'

Sabine's blissfully happy smile was painful to witness. 'Only a little. I'm so glad you two are getting along so well.' She linked her arm through one of Elspeth's and added, 'It will make Fraser's and my wedding day all the more special, won't it, Mack?'

'Indeed it will,' Mack said with a stiff smile that didn't reach the full distance to his eyes. Then he reached for Elspeth's clutch purse off the bookshelf and held it out to her with an enigmatic look. 'You might not want to leave this behind.'

Elspeth was shocked to realise how distracted she had been by him that she had completely forgotten it. Her life depended on the EpiPens in that purse. 'Thank you.' She took her purse from him, only just resisting the urge to snatch it out of his hold. How could she have been so caught up in the moment she had compromised her own safety?

And not just her physical safety. She was beginning to realise Mack MacDiarmid was a threat to her emotional safety.

And sadly, there was no EpiPen for that.

# CHAPTER FOUR

ELSPETH MINGLED WITH the other wedding party guests, trying to make light conversation with one or two of them but all the while aware of Mack's watchful gaze. He seemed to be watching her every movement. Even when she wasn't facing him, she sensed his gaze on her. She had developed a sensitivity where he was concerned, an internal radar that tracked him as assiduously as he tracked her. What did he think she was going to do? Spill all to Sabine about her fiancé's perfidious behaviour? Elspeth was feeling more and more compromised by the situation her twin had placed her in. Elodie had the chutzpah to wing her way through just about any scenario but Elspeth did not.

Firstly, she hadn't had much of a social life over the years due to fears over her allergy, and secondly, she had zero experience in handling men like Mack MacDiarmid. But that didn't stop her being drawn to him as if by some wickedly mischievous magnetic force.

Once the rehearsal was over, the guests were led into one of the grand formal dining rooms for a lavish dinner. Elspeth saw from the beautifully calligraphed nametags on the table that she was seated next to Mack, opposite Fraser and Sabine. She was so nauseated by Fraser's act of loving fiancé eagerly looking forward to his wedding day, she knew she wouldn't be able to eat the dinner even if she weren't worried about nut contamination.

But then, Elspeth knew she was equally guilty in her own game of charades, which unsettled her all the more. Every moment was filled with a sense of dread she would somehow forget she was pretending to be her twin. The fallout would be crucifying, mortifying and horrifying. But even more so, she hated the thought of upsetting the lovely Sabine. The bride-to-be had been nothing but warm and friendly towards her, and yes, perhaps Sabine was a little star-struck by Elodie's fame, but behind that Elspeth could see Sabine's genuine affection for her twin.

A wave of self-doubt washed over her. But she *wasn't* her twin. Was she doing a good enough job of being Elodie? Her twin would have been working the room, smiling at everyone with confidence, charming every man within her orbit. She wouldn't be standing to one side, wondering with a sinking feeling in her stomach how on earth she was going to get through the next couple of hours.

Mack came up beside her at the dining table and pulled out her chair with a smile. 'It seems we're destined to spend more and more time together this weekend.' His eyes contained a teasing glint.

Elspeth sent him a look that threatened to wither the whimsical floral arrangement on the table. 'I can assure you, the prospect doesn't thrill me one little bit.'

His smile tilted a little further and the glint in his gaze sharpened as if he was secretly relishing her sense of discomfiture. 'By the way—' he leaned down to speak close to the shell of her ear and a shiver tumbled down her spine '—I spoke to the chef and gave him strict instructions that your meal is not to be contaminated with nuts.'

Elspeth glanced up at him, her pulse still racing at his closeness. 'That was very…' she disguised a little gulp '…thoughtful of you.' And crazy of her not to have done so herself. How could she expect to sit through a formal dinner without eating a morsel without drawing attention to herself? And how could Mack have such a potent effect on her that he made her forget the one thing that had dominated every day of her life since she was two years old?

'He was totally unaware of your dietary needs,' Mack continued. 'Do you think you should've said something earlier to Sabine or the wedding planner so the caterers could be better prepared?'

'It was on my list of things to do but I got distracted by…other things…' Elspeth knew her reply sounded as unconvincing as it was for someone suffering a life-threatening allergy. But then, her twin didn't have an allergy and suddenly making a fuss about dietary requirements was only going to draw the sort of attention to herself she was hoping to avoid. The sort of attention Mack Mac-Diarmid was focussing on her now, as if he was trying to solve a perplexing puzzle. His brow was furrowed, his gaze slightly narrowed, his expression a landscape of deep concentration.

Sabine and Fraser came to their seats opposite and Elspeth couldn't help noticing the beads of perspiration beading across Fraser's forehead. He looked as if he had been imbibing a little heavily—his cheeks were ruddy and his eyes glassy and his movements a little uncoordinated—although it seemed he was doing all he could to disguise it. It occurred to her how different the two brothers were in temperament and behaviour. Mack was all about emotional regulation, steely control and steadiness. But his younger brother was wayward, reckless and self-indulgent with a lot less ability to control his impulses.

Elspeth couldn't help wondering what Sabine saw in Fraser, what qualities she was drawn to in him. Or had love planted a pair of rose-coloured glasses on her nose? One day those glasses would have to come off, and then what? Poor Sabine would have to face the truth about the man she married.

Sabine reached for Fraser's hand and smiled at him in a loving manner. 'Can you believe that this time tomorrow we'll be husband and wife?'

Fraser's answering smile was a little shaky around the edges. 'I can't wait, my love.' He picked up his champagne glass and raised it in a toast. 'To my beautiful bride-to-be, Sabine. My soulmate, the love of my life.'

Everyone chorused in. 'To Sabine.'

Elspeth wanted to vomit and, judging from

the brief covert glance Mack shared with her, she wasn't the only one.

Later that night when the other guests had gone to bed, Mack stood in front of the windows of one of the smaller sitting rooms overlooking the loch. The moon cast long slim silver beams of light across the smooth glassy surface of the water. Such a tranquil scene to observe given the mental turmoil he currently was experiencing. He still couldn't make Elodie out and it deeply troubled him. Alarm bells were ringing in his head and he trusted his gut enough to know they were ringing for good reason.

But what was the reason?

Elodie Campbell apparently had a life-threatening nut allergy but had not notified the catering staff. There was no mention anywhere online of her having an allergy, only dyslexia, which was another red flag to him given her avid interest in his library. For someone who had struggled to read for most of her life, why then would rare books hold such appeal?

But it was the allergy that rang the biggest alarm bell. Why would she risk something like that? Caterers were trained to be able to handle specific food allergies—all she had to do was inform them. Was she really so concerned about her image that she would put her life in danger? And if she was such a risk-taker and the troublemaker the press and his younger brother made her out to be, why then hadn't she hinted at the one-night stand she'd had with Fraser over dinner? She'd had ample opportunity, not just at dinner but from the moment she'd arrived, and yet she looked as uncomfortable and on edge as Mack felt. Did she intend to sabotage the wedding at some point? Was that her goal, to wait for a moment when the impact of her revelation would be most explosive? Or were his brother's concerns more a reflection of his own guilt and nothing to do with Elodie, who had slept with him supposedly before knowing he was engaged?

Mack preferred to see Elodie as innocent, unknowingly caught up in a drama of his brother's making. But why was *he* so intent on trying to whitewash her reputation? He would be lying if he didn't admit he was attracted to her. Attracted to her in a way he hadn't been towards a woman in a long time, if ever. She was beguiling, bewitching, beautiful and at times completely befuddling, and yet he couldn't get her out of his mind. Her touch had stirred a sensual storm in his body. Every time she came within touching distance, he ached to be even closer. He had come close to kissing her in the library. Every cell in his body had throbbed with the desire to press his lips to her bee-stung ones, to see if they were as soft and responsive as they looked. And yet, she had acted so shocked when he told her he wanted to kiss her. As if she couldn't believe he could possibly be attracted to her. But what was so shocking about that? Men all over the world lusted after her, including his own brother. Surely it hadn't been false modesty on her part. She'd looked positively stunned by his confession. Besides, he'd sensed her attraction to him on more than one occasion. Was she acting coy and shy in order to ramp up the heat? If so, it was working a treat. He was hot for her, all right. Smoking hot.

The problem was—what was he going to do about it?

Under normal circumstances, Elspeth would have quite enjoyed the morning's preparations with the bride and the other bridesmaids under the expert ministrations of the hair and make-up team. She got a tiny glimpse of what her twin experienced in her life as a lingerie model. The pampering, the priming, the professional grooming had turned her into a stunning version of herself. Her skin glowed, her hair was expertly assembled in an up-do that highlighted her cheekbones and the slim length of her neck. The oyster silk bridesmaid dress was slim-fitting with shoestring shoulder straps, and the unusual mushroom colour worked surprisingly well with the smoky tones of her eyeshadow.

Sabine looked exquisite in a diaphanous white cloud of a designer off-the-shoulder dress, the cinched-in waist emphasising her womanly curves. The voluminous veil had a long train that made her look like a fairy-tale princess. Her face shone with happiness and her eyes with excitement. She glanced at the slim watch on her wrist—the borrowed item, from her grandmother. 'Right. It's time to go. I've made him wait long enough. Ready, girls?'

'We're ready,' the other bridesmaids chorused.

The wisteria walk where the ceremony was to be conducted was in full bloom, the scent intoxicating. Elspeth was aware of a creeping anxiety, no doubt triggered by the memories of her twin's ill-fated wedding day. Although her twin's ceremony had been in a church, a cathedral at that, with rows and rows of guests, the atmosphere was the same. The almost palpable sense of expectation from the gathered guests, the chamber music eerily playing exactly the same piece, the groom and groomsmen dressed magnificently in full Highland apparel, including kilts, waiting for the bride and her attendants to appear.

The bride was standing with her father behind a screen, waiting for the moment to come forward, once the bridesmaids had begun their progression.

Before she began to walk forward, Elspeth glanced back to see Sabine's father frowning as he talked to his daughter. It didn't seem like the sort of conversation a father and daughter should be having just moments from walking up the aisle. Why wasn't he smiling at his daughter with pride? Why was he looking so grave and serious? His hand was on her arm in a stalling gesture. His voice was pitched low but was still loud enough for Elspeth to hear her sister's name mentioned. A wave of panic flooded her being, a cold hand of dread gripped her insides and her knees began to knock together.

Sabine's expression suddenly folded and her gaze sought Elspeth's. 'Is it true?' she asked in a shocked tone. 'Oh, God, is it true you slept with Fraser?'

Elspeth opened and closed her mouth; her throat so dry she could barely get her voice to work. 'It's not what you think—'

Sabine thrust her beautiful bouquet towards one of the other bridesmaids and stalked towards Elspeth, the click-clacking of her heels on the flagstones as loud as gunshots. 'My dad assures me it *is* true. He overheard one of the groomsmen, Tim, ribbing Fraser about it when they were having a pre-ceremony whisky a few minutes ago. It was when Fraser was in London a few months back.' She narrowed her eyes to paper-thin slits. 'How *could* you? How could you be so crass as to agree to be my bridesmaid when you slept with my fiancé?' Her voice had become a screech, and there was a rumble of concern from the gathered guests on the other side of the screen.

Elspeth took a step backwards; worried Sabine might lash out at her. 'Sabine, please let me explain. It wasn't me… I mean, I—I didn't know he was engaged. He didn't tell me…we barely exchanged names before we…' she winced in embarrassment on behalf of her twin as well as herself and stumbled on '…hooked up. It meant nothing to either of us.'

'Well, it means something to *me*,' Sabine stormed back, eyes blazing. She turned to her father. 'Tell Fraser the wedding is off. I never want to see him again.' She turned back to Elspeth and added, 'And that applies to you too. I thought you were my friend but the whole time you've been acting, haven't you? You probably don't even like me.'

Elspeth had been acting but not the way Sabine thought. 'I—I really like you, Sabine. You deserve far better than Fraser. I'm sorry it happened this way but, believe me, I'm really not the problem here—the problem is Fraser's lack of fidelity. If it hadn't been with…with me, it could've been someone else.' It *had* been someone else, Elspeth desperately wanted to add but couldn't without betraying her twin. Was this what Elodie was hoping to avoid by sending Elspeth in her place? Had Elodie suspected something like this was going to happen? Sabine's father was a wealthy and savvy businessman and Sabine was his only child. No wonder he had informed Sabine of her fiancé's indiscretion before the marriage could take place.

Mack suddenly appeared and took Elspeth by the arm just as Fraser came rushing over, pleading with Sabine to listen to him. 'Sabine, my love. What are you doing? You know you're the only woman I love. Don't do this.'

Sabine let out a piercing wail and flung herself against her father's chest. 'Send him away. I never want to see him or that ghastly woman again.'

'Come with me,' Mack said, leading Elspeth away by the elbow.

She followed him in a numb silence, her stomach churning so much she could have made enough butter to supply Scotland's biggest shortbread factory. As much as Elspeth was glad Sabine wasn't going to marry Fraser, she hated that 'she' was to blame. How could her twin have put her in such a compromising situation? It was beyond embarrassing, not to mention laughably ironic. Elspeth, acting as her twin, was being portrayed as 'the other woman' when she had never had sex in her life.

Mack led her to his study on one of the upper floors well away from the central part of the castle. He closed the door once they were inside and let out a long breath, his expression difficult to read. 'Well, you achieved your aim. The wedding is off.' One ink-black eyebrow hooked upwards and he continued.

'It seems to be a habit of yours, calling off weddings at the last moment.'

'I—I'm not responsible for what just happened.' Elspeth tried to keep her voice steady but it was as shaky as her hands. She was still carrying her bridesmaid bouquet but, because her hands were trembling so much, petals were falling like confetti around her.

'Maybe not directly, but you said you didn't think he was good enough for Sabine. Does that mean you want him for yourself?' This time there was no mistaking his expression—it was dark and brooding.

Elspeth coughed out a startled cynical laugh. 'You must be joking.'

'I'm not.' The blunt edge to his tone sent a chill down her spine.

She turned away to put the bouquet down on his desk and chewed at the edge of her mouth. If only she could tell him the truth. If only Elodie had got here in time, she wouldn't be experiencing the most distressing episode of her entire life. Anaphylaxis was a piece of cake compared to this. She kept her back to Mack, her hands gripping the edge of his desk to steady her wobbly legs. 'I can assure you I have no interest whatsoever in your brother.'

Mack came up behind her and placed his

hands on the tops of her shoulders. A thrill ran through her body and her heart picked up its pace. He turned her slowly to face him, his eyes locking on hers. 'Are you okay?'

'No, I'm not okay. Did you see how mad Sabine was? I thought she was going to slap me. I don't like the thought of her hating me so much. I really like her. She's a nice person and to have her wedding day ruined in such a way is just awful. Why did her father tell her just then, right before she was going to walk down the aisle? If only he had found out earlier then she wouldn't have had to go through such dreadful public humiliation.' Tears stung at the backs of her eyes and she furiously blinked them away and bit down on her lower lip.

One tear managed to escape and Mack blotted it away with the pad of his thumb. 'You really care about Sabine?'

'Of course. This was supposed to be the happiest day of her life and now it's completely ruined.'

Mack gave the tops of her shoulders a gentle squeeze. 'I want you to wait for me here. I'll get one of the servants to pack your things. I don't want this to blow up in the press. Hopefully, I can talk some sense into Sabine and—'

'Hang on a minute,' Elspeth cut across him and wriggled out of his hold, taking a couple of steps back. 'Are you saying you still want her to marry your brother, even though she's made her position perfectly clear?'

His jaw tightened like a clamp. 'Do you have any idea of how much this weekend cost?'

'So, it's about the money?' She rolled her eyes in disdain. 'What about what's right for Sabine? Your brother stuffed up and now it's time he faced up to the consequences.'

Mack let out a hefty sigh, one of his hands scraping through his hair, leaving it sexily tousled. 'It's not about the money.' His voice sounded weary, weighted. 'Fraser won't handle a breakup like this. Sabine has been good for him. She's been a positive influence on him over the last couple of years. He's been happier with her than I've seen him with anyone else in years, possibly ever.'

Elspeth folded her arms and sent him a cynical look. 'So happy, he hooked up with a woman he had never met before in London, without telling her he was already engaged. Yes, I can see how blissfully happy he must've been.'

Mack twisted his mouth. 'I'm sorry you've been caught up in the middle of this. He was wrong not to tell you his relationship status.' He moved to the other side of the room, his hand rubbing at the back of his neck as if trying to release a knot of tension. He let out another deep sigh. 'Fraser took our father's death hard. He was only fourteen—I was sixteen—and it threw him completely, as it did all of us.' He sent her a bleak glance. 'I tried to be a good role model for him but clearly that didn't work. He's reckless and impulsive and refuses to face up to responsibility. In many ways, he's very like our father, which is worrying.'

Elspeth frowned. 'How did your father die?'

'Suicide.' He swallowed deeply and continued. 'Our mother found him. She had a nervous breakdown after that. She was never quite the same. She died five years later of cancer, which, of course, sent Fraser into another massive tailspin. But meeting Sabine a couple of years ago changed everything for him. He started to pull himself into line. He got a job with her father's company and he really applied himself. He gave up the wild partying, the party drugs. But now…' He shook his head and frowned as if he couldn't quite believe what had happened in the garden just minutes before.

'You think he'll go back to that lifestyle?'

Mack gave her a world-weary look. 'What do you think?'

'I don't know your brother well enough to speculate.' Elspeth's cheeks grew uncomfortably warm as she thought of how Mack must view her statement given 'she' had supposedly had a one-night stand with him. 'But I'm thinking Sabine's father isn't going to want him working for him.'

'Got it in one.'

Elspeth could only imagine the stress Mack must have gone through over the loss of his father and then the breakdown of his mother and subsequent acting out of his younger brother. And all while he was sixteen, only two years older than his brother. 'How did you cope with the loss of your father? I mean, it must have been so hard for you too.'

Mack's expression became masked and she realised then how he coped—by concealing his own struggles, his own deep distress. He was resilient, self-reliant, stoic. 'I grew up fast. I had to. There was no one else to take charge.'

'No grandparents?'

'My paternal grandparents died when I was four. Car crash. I can barely remember them now. Fraser can't remember them at all.'

'And your mother's parents?'

'My mother's mother died when she was thirteen. Breast cancer, the same cancer that got her. Her father died when I was ten. I have lots of fond memories of him. He was a good man, steady and reliable.'

'Like you.'

Mack shrugged one broad shoulder in a dismissive manner. 'Someone has to be steady in a crisis, which brings me back to the plan.'

'The plan?'

'The press are going to swarm around you like hornets, so you need to go to ground. Immediately.'

Elspeth gripped the back of an oak chair to steady her suddenly trembling legs. 'The press?'

'The paparazzi. One whiff of this and you'll be hounded for an exclusive tell-all interview. But I should warn you against giving one.'

Elspeth swallowed. The thought of the

press hounding her, chasing her, thrusting microphones and cameras in her face terrified her. 'I would never do that.'

One dark eyebrow winged upwards. 'I'm afraid I can't afford to believe you, so I will be accompanying you until this blows over.'

Elspeth gawped at him. Had she heard him correctly? 'Accompanying me? Accompanying me where?'

'To a secret hideaway.'

'You're...*kidnapping* me?' Her eyes were so round they threatened to pop out of her head. Could this farce get any more ridiculous?

He gave a light laugh. 'Ever the drama queen. No, I'm giving you a choice. You either come with me willingly or I leave you to face the destruction of your reputation and quite possibly your career.'

Elspeth's heart skipped a beat. Two beats. And then went into a wacky rhythm as if she were suffering some sort of serious cardiac condition. 'That sounds suspiciously like blackmail to me.'

'Think of it as a choice.'

She put her chin up and eyeballed him. 'Your way or the highway?'

His smile was indolent but his grey-blue

gaze was steely with determination. 'I believe it's in your best interests to come with me.'

'For how long?'

'One night until the guests and the paps leave. But longer if necessary.'

'Longer? But what about my job? I can't just disappear without warning.' He wasn't to know she had already taken next week off work to have a look around Scotland to visit some of the villages her family's ancestors came from. And as to what engagements her twin had for the next few days, well, Elspeth needed to find a private room to call Elodie to tell her what was going on. Elodie would have to go into hiding too, until this scandal blew over. *If* it blew over.

'I'm sure you can take time off work but I'll reimburse you for any lost wages.'

No way did she want to face the paparazzi.

No way did she want to face the wrath of poor heartbroken Sabine.

And no way did she want to miss out on a night in hiding with Mack. Why shouldn't she go with him? It would be a perfect opportunity to see how the other half lived. This was her chance, maybe her only chance, to live a little dangerously. And it didn't get more deliciously dangerous than spending time with devilishly handsome Mack Mac-Diarmid.

'So now you're bribing me?'

'Is it working?'

Elspeth gave him the side eye. 'A little too well.'

# CHAPTER FIVE

MACK GAVE ONE of the most discreet of his household staff directions on packing up Elodie's things and transferring them to his car, along with food and drink for an overnight stay. He then tracked down his brother in his suite of rooms. Fraser was pacing the floor and swung to face Mack as he came in.

'You have to talk to Sabine, Mack. You have to convince her to change her mind. Her father's threatening to pull the plug on my career. I need to get her to reconsider, otherwise I'm doomed. That crazy Campbell bitch is behind this, I just know it. It's why she agreed to be bridesmaid.' He clenched his fists, his expression thunderous. 'She wanted this to happen. She planned it from the start.'

Mack was having trouble aligning his view of Elodie with that of his brother. It was as if they were talking about two different people. The Elodie he'd spent time with was feisty at times, yes, but underneath that was a warm and sweet person who seemed to care about others more than she did herself.

*Two different people...*

The thought got a little more traction in his mind. Those alarm bells had rung and rung and rung inside his head until he was almost deaf with the sound of them. Why hadn't he thought of it before? The answer was so obvious. What if he was dealing with two different people? Was it possible the young woman he had almost kissed in the library yesterday, the young woman he had convinced to go away with him overnight, was not the real Elodie Campbell? He whipped out his phone, pointedly ignoring his brother's continued ranting, and quickly did a search of press releases about Elodie Campbell's called-off wedding. His search proved fruitless until he typed in Lincoln Lancaster's name and then a couple of articles loaded, one with a picture. He stared at the grainy image of three bridesmaids gathered outside the church. One of them had her face slightly turned away but Mack would recognise that profile anywhere. The younger sister of Elodie Campbell was not just a younger sister but a twin. An identical twin.

'Are you listening to me?' Fraser said. 'I

said I need you to talk to Sabine. Tell her she's making a terrible mistake.'

Mack put his phone in his jacket pocket. He decided to keep his new discovery to himself a little bit longer. He wanted to find out the reason for the switch, wanted to understand the motivations behind the decision to stand in for her twin. Wanted to know how far the beautiful little imposter was going to take this charade. 'I'm inclined to agree with Sabine. If she married you, it would be her making the terrible mistake.'

'How can you say that? I love her.'

'You don't love her. You love how she made you feel. She worshipped you, got her father to give you a great job, told you all the things your male ego wanted to hear. But you don't love her. If you did, you wouldn't have betrayed her.'

'It was Elodie Campbell's fault. I wouldn't have looked twice at her but she—'

'I'm tired of hearing how it's always everyone else's fault when you stuff up,' Mack said. 'I can't fix this for you, Fraser. This is your mess and for once I'm not going to untangle it for you.' He had been doing way too much enabling of his brother, he realised now. Stepping in when he should have stepped back. His fears over Fraser taking the path of their father were real fears but he couldn't spend his life babysitting his younger brother. The cancelled wedding was a huge wake-up call for Fraser and if Mack tried to intervene, it might lessen the impact. It was time for his brother to grow up and take responsibility for the mess he had made.

Besides, Mack had a little mess of his own to untangle.

While Mack went to see about the transfer of her luggage to his car, Elspeth took the opportunity to call her twin. 'Elodie? You'll never guess what happened.'

'I was about to call you. I just saw it on social media,' Elodie said. 'Whatever you do, don't say anything to the press. God, I don't need this right now.'

'But what about me?' Elspeth said. 'I'm still pretending to be you. How long do you think I can keep this up?'

'You can come home any time you like now the wedding's been called off. But you'll have to lie low, and, come to think of it, so will I.'

'Well, here's the thing—Mack MacDiarmid is insisting I go away with him overnight.'

There was a short silence.

'And you said yes?' Elodie's tone was incredulous.

'You're always telling me I need to be more adventurous, so that's what I'm going to do. Go with the flow.'

'But you're going as me, right?'

'Well, yes, because I can't exactly tell him I'm not you now, can I?' Elspeth couldn't imagine how she could ever reveal her true identity to Mack. Not after all the lies she had told. No, she would go away with Mack and enjoy the little adventure for what it was—a chance to live a little before she went back to her normal quiet life.

'No, I guess not but it's kind of tricky...' Elodie's tone contained a note of something Elspeth hadn't heard in it before.

'Tricky in what way?'

'What if the press see you together? I mean, while you're pretending to be me?'

Elspeth frowned. 'Hello? You're the one who insisted I stand in for you at a society wedding, remember? Heaps of photos have been taken all weekend, so—'

'Yes, but if you're having a one-night stand with Mack MacDiarmid, then—'

'I'm not having any such thing with him. He's just keen to keep me away from the press.'

'But you're seriously tempted.' Her twin stated it rather than posed it as a question.

Elspeth tried to ignore the little flutter of excitement in her belly. 'He's a very attractive man and, besides, you're always telling me I need to get out more. This is my chance to live a little.'

'But I can't be seen to be cavorting with Mack MacDiarmid right now,' Elodie insisted.

'Who's going to see you, I mean me?'

'Anyone with a camera phone, that's who. The media pay enormous sums for those photos these days and they often go viral. It could be very compromising for me.'

'Because of your financial backer?'

'That and...other things.'

'What other things?'

'Never mind. Just keep a low profile. And whatever you do, don't tell Mack who you really are. He might not take too kindly to having been hoodwinked by you.'

Elspeth quailed at the thought of revealing her true identity to Mack. While she sensed he had a good sense of humour, somehow she didn't think he would find her switching places with her twin all that amusing. Especially as it had brought about the cancellation of his brother's wedding, an event Mack had been determined would go ahead no matter what. 'Don't worry, I won't.'

A short time later, Mack helped Elspeth into a four-wheel-drive vehicle, and then drove, not out through the castle gates, as she was expecting, but deeper into the estate.

She glanced at him in confusion. 'Where are we going? Is there a back exit to the estate?'

Mack sent her an unreadable look. 'Not unless we climb over the Highlands on foot. There's an old crofter's hut up in the hills. We can hide out there overnight until the press leave. They won't find us there.'

'An old crofter's hut. Wow. That sounds kind of rustic.'

'It is.' He sent her another sideways glance. 'You won't find the lack of five-star accommodation off-putting?'

'No, it'll be like stepping back in time.' Not to mention right out of her comfort zone. But not because of the lack of creature comforts. Elspeth could barely believe she was agreeing to this—being spirited away to a secluded spot on the estate to be alone with Mack. To draw the attention away from her fluttering nerves she redirected the conversation. 'Did you speak to your brother? How's he handling things?'

He let out a deep sigh and adjusted the gears to drive over a deep pothole on the gravel road. She couldn't stop staring at his hands, so strong and competent on the gear stick and steering wheel as he negotiated the rough passage. No doubt they were just as competent moving over a woman's body. She suppressed a little shiver at the thought of his hands on her body. 'He's blaming you for everything.'

Elspeth bit down on her lower lip and glanced at the deep green forest on the left side of the car. 'And what about you? Do you blame me too?'

'Not at all.' There was something in his tone that made her glance at him but his expression was masklike.

'You're not angry the wedding didn't go ahead? I mean, it must have cost a bomb to host it and all...'

His mouth twisted in a rueful manner. 'The money isn't the issue. I'm inclined to agree with you now that I've thought about it. Fraser isn't the right person for Sabine. He's not the right person for anyone and won't be until he does some serious work on himself.' He shifted the gears again and the car rocked from side to side as it went over another deep ridge. 'And he won't do the work if I keep stepping in and making things too easy for him.'

'I'm sure you've always done what you thought is best for your brother.'

Mack sent her a grim look. 'You're being way too generous. No, I've made plenty of mistakes with Fraser.' His knuckles turned white on the steering wheel and his jaw tightened. 'I sometimes wonder if our father hadn't died the way he did, would Fraser have turned out differently?' A shadow passed across his face like the scudding clouds across the sky.

Elspeth placed a gentle hand on his thigh, compelled to offer her support and comfort. 'You're a wonderful older brother, Mack. Anyone can see that. And don't forget you were only young yourself when your father died. And you lost your mother so soon after that. Sometimes people are the way they are, not so much because of circumstances but because of how they deal with the circumstances. And maybe that has more to do with personality than anything else.'

Mack placed his hand over the top of hers and gave it a gentle squeeze. Tingles raced up her arm like lightning, sending a wave of heat to her core. 'You're nothing like the press make you out to be. I was expecting a spoilt prima donna.'

Elspeth pulled her hand out from under his and laid it in her lap before she was tempted to let it explore further along his muscled thigh. 'I—I've encouraged a certain view of myself,' she said, recalling a conversation with her twin about building Elodie's brand. Smart, sassy, sophisticated, sexy— four words that certainly applied to her twin but not to her. 'But it's a public persona, it's not the real me.'

'As I've found out.' There was a cryptic quality to his tone that sent a shiver cartwheeling down her spine. She chanced a glance at him but his expression was difficult to read, although she did happen to notice a twinkling light in his eyes.

They travelled a little way further before they came to a fast-running stream coursing across rocks. 'Hold on,' Mack said, shifting the gears again.

Elspeth gripped the edges of her seat and held her breath as Mack expertly guided the vehicle across the stream. 'You're really making sure no one can follow us, aren't you?'

He gave her a heart-stopping grin and

gunned the engine up the steep slope on the other side. 'That's the idea, *m'eudail.*'

A few minutes later, Mack pulled up outside an old crofter's hut that was situated at the top of the rise with views across a deep valley. Elspeth was out of the vehicle before he could get to her door. She stood, taking in the spectacular view, the crisp cool air so fresh she could almost taste it. A wedge-tailed eagle freewheeled on the air currents above, the eerie sound of his call echoing across the valley. A stag deer raised its head in the distance, his giant antlers looking too heavy for him to carry. He returned to cropping the grass as if used to seeing Mack show up.

'Oh, my goodness, it's so beautiful...' Elspeth gasped in wonder. 'It's a wonder you can bear to live anywhere else...'

Mack stood behind her, his hands going to the tops of her shoulders in a touch as light as the air she was breathing but it still sent a delicious shock wave through her body. Just knowing his tall frame was so close to her made her heart race and her pulse pound.

He quoted in a broad Scots brogue. '"*My heart's in the Highlands, my heart is not here; My heart's in the Highlands, a-chasing the deer. Chasing the wild-deer, and fol-*

*lowing the roe. My heart's in the Highlands, wherever I go."'*

Elspeth turned to look up at him with a smile. 'Robert Burns says it so well.' But inside, she was thinking of another Robert Burns quote that reminded her of the fine line she was walking. *'The best laid schemes o' mice an' men Gang aft agley. An'lea'e us nought but grief an' pain. For promis'd joy.'*

He gave an answering smile that made her heart flutter. 'I'm glad you like it here.' His voice was low and deep and rough.

'How could I not? It's the most stunning place I've ever been to.' Eek! Elspeth suddenly remembered all the stunning locations her twin had been to. Photos of Elodie were all over the Internet, posing beside spectacular views of mountains, beaches, rainforests—you name it, Elodie had been there. Would he pick up on her slip?

Mack's hands went to her hips, holding her within a hair's breadth from his powerful male body. 'But you've been to so many exotic locations for your work, have you not? This must hardly compare.' His gaze was unwavering and it made her heart beat all the harder and she could feel her cheeks heating up in spite of the cool Highland breeze.

'This is the sort of place I love the most,'

Elspeth said, conscious of heat crawling over her face. 'It's so peaceful and timeless. If you look out there—' she pointed to the view across the valley '—there's nothing to anchor you to this century. We could be from any time in the past. Don't you find that amazing?'

Mack framed her face in his large hands, his gaze dipping to her mouth. 'What I find amazing is how I've resisted kissing you until now. Would you mind?'

Elspeth licked her lips with a nervous flick of her tongue. 'No… I mean yes, I want you to kiss me.'

His mouth came down to press against hers in a feather-light touchdown. He lifted his lips off hers and came down again, a little firmer this time as if driven by a pounding need for closer contact. The same pounding need that was barrelling through her own body. She gave a soft little whimper and linked her arms around his neck, opening her lips to the commanding probe of his tongue. Heat exploded inside her, molten heat that travelled to the centre of her womanhood, moistening and swelling tender tissues as primal need took over.

Mack groaned and angled his head for deeper access, one of his hands sliding into the thickness of her hair. 'I've wanted to do this from the moment I met you.' He growled against her lips.

Elspeth planted a series of short hot kisses to his lips. 'What took you so long?'

He smiled against her lips. 'You have no idea how much I wanted to kiss you in the library.'

She leaned against his masculine frame, her insides coiling with lust as she came into contact with the hardened ridge of his erection. 'What stopped you?'

Mack lifted his head a fraction and stroked a lazy finger across her lower lip. 'I wanted to get to know you better first.'

*You don't know me at all.*

Elspeth wished she could tell him the truth about her identity. It seemed wrong that he thought she was Elodie. That he *thought* he was kissing Elodie. But the risks of confessing her true identity were too great. It would create an even bigger scandal, even more hurt for Sabine, who would feel betrayed all over again.

Elspeth traced a line around his sculptured lips. 'How well do you think you know me?' She couldn't get her voice above a thready whisper.

He took the end of her finger into his mouth,

sucking on it gently, his gaze holding hers. A hot shiver raced like greased lightning down her back, heat smouldering in her core at the erotic intention in the caress. 'Well enough to know you want me as much as I want you.'

Elspeth suppressed a frisson of delight, her gaze locked on his by a force as old as time. 'I've never wanted anyone like I want you.'

He smiled a slow smile and cradled one side of her face in his hand. 'Same. So, what are we going to do about it?'

She licked her lips again, tasting the sexy salt of him, wanting him with an ache that throbbed like pain. 'I guess we could kiss again and see what happens.'

'Sounds like a good plan.' His mouth came back down to hers in a blistering kiss that made the hairs on her head stand up on tip-toe. His tongue entered her mouth in a brazen thrust that sent a hot dart of need to her feminine core. Her pulse picked up its pace, her blood thrumming with primal want, her mouth feeding off his as if it were her only lifeline.

He made a guttural sound and deepened the kiss, his tongue tangling with hers in a sexy tango that fuelled her desire even more. One of his hands went to the small of her back, pressing her closer to the potent heat of his male form. A delicious shudder went through her at the erotic contact, her body secretly preparing itself for his possession. Aching for his possession as if it had been waiting all these years for this exact moment.

Mack raised his head after a few breathless moments, his eyes glazed with lust. 'Let's take this indoors. I want our first time to be without mosquitoes and prickling heather.'

Our first time…

*My first time…*

Elspeth disguised a gulping swallow. 'Right…'

He captured her chin between his finger and thumb, his gaze suddenly searching. 'Is something wrong?'

How could she tell him it would be her first time without revealing her deception? If she confessed, he might pull the plug on their sensual encounter. How could she sabotage something she wanted so much? She was aching for him from head to foot, need pulsing inside every cell of her body. The need for him. *Only* him. He had awakened something in her and she couldn't bear to deny her body the satisfaction it craved. She schooled her features into a mask of confidence while inside her nerves were fluttering like frenzied moths. 'Nothing. It's just been a while since I… I got with a guy…' Her burning cheeks could have started a grass fire.

'You mean not since my brother?'

'Erm…can we not talk about that?'

'Sure.' Mack stroked a finger down the curve of her hot cheek. 'You don't need to be nervous. I'm nothing like my brother.'

*And I'm nothing like my sister.*

'I—I'm not nervous…'

He brushed her lips with his in a light as air kiss, his taste delighting her all over again. 'I'm not going to rush you. We'll get unpacked and have a drink to relax first. It's been quite a day.'

Elspeth didn't know whether to be relieved or disappointed. She didn't need a drink—she needed him. Badly. 'Yes, it has.'

The crofter's hut was built on one level and made of local stone. While a little larger than some she had seen in books, it still had a quaint and timeless atmosphere. It was tastefully and respectfully renovated inside with a fireplace in the kitchen-cum-living-area as well as in the bedroom. And to her very great relief, there was even a small bathroom off the bedroom.

'Do you come up here often?' Elspeth asked, wondering how many women he had brought here for a private tryst.

Mack placed her bag on the floor near the bed. 'As often as I can when I'm home. It's my thinking space. I started to come up here after my father died. Like everything else on the estate, it was pretty run-down back then but over time I was able to fix things up.'

She perched on the edge of the bed, her hands clasped in her lap—a combination of nerves and an attempt at fighting the temptation to reach for him. 'You were named after him, weren't you? Sabine mentioned it when we were getting our hair and make-up done. But you don't get called Robert.'

'No.' He flicked a bit of imaginary dust off a side table. 'I was Robbie when I was a young child but everyone started calling me Mack during my early teens. It was assumed I'd go back to my father's name after his death but it never appealed to me. I stuck with Mack.'

'You wanted to distance yourself from him?'

He gave her a grim look. 'You don't get any more distant than death but that was his choice.'

Elspeth chewed her lower lip, wondering if he had ever dealt with the grief of losing his father in such a sudden and tragic way. He had had to step up and deal with the fallout from his father's death. He wouldn't have had time to process his own feelings, especially with his younger brother acting out and his mother needing so much emotional support. 'Maybe he didn't feel he had a choice at that point in his life. Things can seem so hopeless for a moment in time but even seconds later, things can look completely different. People talk about looking for the light at the end of the tunnel but life is not always a straight tunnel but more like a winding one. You can't see around the next bend but you have to hope that something good is waiting there for you. And if the good thing isn't around that bend, then you hope the next or the next will have it.'

Mack blew out a long sigh, his expression darkly shadowed. 'He lied to my face so many times. Blatant lies that I've gone over in my head ever since, wondering why he couldn't be honest. He ruined so many lives—my mother's, his lover's and their child's. Not to mention Fraser's. I can't help wondering if Fraser would have turned to drink and drugs if our father had just ended his marriage instead of his life. It was so unnecessary. We would have got over his affair, even my mother would have handled that, but it was the years and years of lies that hurt the most. And then his death. The finality of it, the fallout from it.' He shook his head, his eyes scrunched up as if in acute pain. 'Mum was never the same. I often wonder if my father thought of that when he...' He swallowed and continued in a ragged tone. 'I guess I have to be thankful it wasn't Fraser who found him, or Daisy, his little daughter.'

Elspeth's conscience was in agony, griping with agonising pain and guilt at all the lies she had told. How could she ever tell Mack who she really was? Lies had ruined his family, torn it apart in the most brutal way. He was still dealing with the fallout of his father's death by trying to keep his brother on the right path. He had lost both his parents within the space of a few short years and yet he had carried on stoically, doing all he could to save his ancestral home from being sold. But at what price to himself? Was that why he was a love-them-and-leave-them playboy? He didn't allow anyone under his guard. He didn't fall in love, in fact, believed himself incapable of it.

'Oh, Mack...' Elspeth rose from where she was perched on the end of the bed and went over to him, touching him on the forearm. 'I'm so sorry you had to deal with such dreadful heartache. But I admire you so much for staying strong for everyone else. For taking control when things were flung so wildly out of control.'

Mack lifted her chin with a gentle finger, his expression rueful. 'You're wasting yourself as a lingerie model, you know. You should be a counsellor.'

Elspeth shifted her gaze to study his firm chin where pinpricks of dark stubble were sprouting. 'Yes, well, it's amazing what skills you learn on the catwalk.' She painted a stiff smile on her face. 'You said something about a drink?'

'I'll bring in the supplies from the car. Make yourself comfortable.'

Elspeth let out a long breath once the door shut behind him. How could she ever be comfortable pretending to be someone else? She wanted to be with Mack as herself, not as her twin.

But how could she tell him she had lied to him from the moment she met him?

# CHAPTER SIX

MACK STOOD OUTSIDE the crofter's hut and took in a deep lungful of crisp Highland air. Somehow, unburdening himself to Elspeth had loosened the tight knot of pain deep inside his chest that had lain there for years. And yet, she was still intent on carrying on with her charade. How long did she think she could keep it going? While it was amusing to watch her valiantly act in her twin's persona, he found himself wanting her to confess, especially now they were alone. He wanted her to know he knew exactly who he was kissing. Who he was making love to. That it was increasingly difficult for her to stay in her twin's persona was more than obvious. But it had to be her decision to confess the twin-switch. How far was she prepared to run with it? That she had taken it this far showed a strong commitment to her twin, which was admirable, but what if there was some other motive? Or was he getting too cynical and jaded?

Mack came back to the hut with the box of supplies the housekeeper had organised for him. Elspeth was sitting on the small sofa in front of the fireplace, her legs curled beneath her. She had changed into casual clothes and her hair was loosened from the up-do and cascaded around her shoulders in a red-gold cloud. He wondered if he had ever seen a more beautiful woman. Or a more desirable one. She unfolded herself from the sofa, her graceful movements and slim figure reminding him of a ballerina. 'Do you want some help?'

Mack placed the box on the small kitchen table and began to take out the items. 'It's okay. I'm used to doing this.'

A shadow passed over her face and her small white teeth sank into her lower lip. 'Yes, well, no doubt you've brought dozens of women up here for a secret getaway.'

He placed the bottle of champagne on the table with a soft thud. 'Actually, you're the first person I've brought here.'

A look of astonishment came over her face. 'Really? But why? I mean, why me?'

*Good question.*

One Mack didn't have an answer for her

other than she was the first woman he'd wanted to bring here to his private sanctuary. The first woman he felt would truly appreciate it in the way he did. The raw beauty of it, the isolation and starkness and untouched wildness speaking to his soul as no other place could. 'I wanted to get you away from the press and this seemed a good place. The best place. Only a handful of people know it even exists.'

Elspeth tucked a strand of her hair behind her ear, her cheeks a faint shade of pink. 'I guess I should feel honoured...' Her gaze fell away from his. 'Mack?' Her voice was tentatively soft.

'What's on your mind?'

'Nothing.' Her response was quick. Too quick. Her gaze troubled, her teeth savaging her lip once more, her cheeks a darker shade of pink.

Mack placed a packet of oat crackers on the table next to the cheese and came over to her, taking her by the hands. 'Is there something you want to say to me?'

'Just...thank you for bringing me here. It's a beautiful place and I... I'm glad I don't have to face the press right now. I would've found it too distressing.'

Mack brushed a loose strand of her hair

back from her face. 'But you're used to handling the press.'

She looked down at their joined hands. 'Yes, but this is different…everything about this…about us is different…'

He brought her chin up so her gaze met his once more. 'What's different about us?'

She moistened her lips with the tip of her tongue. 'I'm not really how I'm portrayed in the media. I want you to know that before we…go any further…'

Mack stroked her pink cheek with the broad pad of his thumb, his eyes locked on hers. 'There's another Robert Burns quote I like. *"O wad some Power the giftie gie us To see oursels as ithers see us! It wad frae mony a blunder free us, An' foolish notion."'*

She gave an effigy of a smile. 'So true…'

Mack lowered his mouth to hers in a soft kiss that made his lips tingle and buzz for more. Elspeth sighed against his lips and pressed herself closer, her hands going to the wall of his chest, her lips opening beneath the pressure of his. He wrapped his arms around her, bringing her as close to his aching body as he could. The slim contours of her body exciting him as no other woman had ever done. Need pummelled through him, a pounding, punishing need that drove every other thought out of his mind other than to possess her in order to quell this maddening ache of his flesh.

He kissed her deeply, thoroughly, delighting in the breathless murmurs of encouragement she gave. Her hands moved from his chest to wind around his neck and she stood on tiptoe, bringing her pelvis into blistering contact with his. Mack cupped the sweet curves of her bottom, holding her to his throbbing length, wondering if he had ever felt so aroused before. Something about her shy sensuality stirred his senses into a frenzy. Her body spoke to his in a language as old as the craggy peaks of the Highlands.

Mack placed one of his hands below her right breast, aching to feel the weight of the soft curve in his hand but not wanting to rush her.

Elspeth whispered her approval against his lips. 'Touch me.'

He needed no other encouragement. He gently peeled away her top and lowered the slim strap of her bra to access her breast. He drank in the sight of her before he brought his mouth to the creamy curve with its rosy peak. He caressed her with his lips and tongue, enjoying the sounds of her pleasure as much as he enjoyed the taste of her in his mouth. He moved to her other breast, uncovering it and caressing it with the same sensual focus. He finally raised his mouth off her soft flesh, looking into her lust-glazed eyes. 'I wanted you from the moment I met you.'

She stroked her hand down the length of his jaw. 'That soon?'

He smiled and ran his hands down the sides of her body to bring her hips flush against his. 'You sound surprised.'

'I am.'

Mack ran his hands through the silky thickness of her hair. 'I would have thought you'd be well used to men lusting over you by now.'

Something passed through her gaze like a faint ripple across a body of still water. Her gaze dipped to his mouth, her throat rising and falling over a swallow. 'Mack?'

He tilted her face upwards to meet his gaze. 'Yes?'

She swallowed again and stepped out of his hold, pulling her bra and loose-fitting top back into place. 'I need to tell you something...something about myself that you're not going to like.'

'Go on.'

She shifted her lips from side to side, then

bit down on her lower one. She did it so often, he wondered if she was even conscious of it. 'I've been lying to you from the moment we met.'

'I know.'

She rapid-blinked. 'Pardon?'

Mack gave a lazy smile. 'I was wondering how long you were going to keep it up.'

Her expression was wary. 'Keep what up?'

'The act.'

She licked her lips, her mouth opening and closing. 'The…act?'

Mack came over to her and took her by the upper arms. 'You little goose. How long did you think you could pull it off? You're nothing like your twin apart from in looks.'

A host of emotions washed over her face—shock, relief, surprise, dismay, even a little anger. 'How did you know? *When* did you know?'

'Not until earlier today, although I had my suspicions from my first glimpse of you at the window when you first arrived at Crannochbrae.'

Elspeth pulled away from him and hugged her arms around her body again. 'Does anyone else know?'

'No.'

She began to pace the floor. 'No one can

know, especially not Sabine. She's been hurt enough.' She stopped pacing and arched her head back to look at the ceiling and groaned. 'Argh, why did I allow myself to think I could do this? I knew I would stuff it up.'

'You didn't stuff it up,' Mack said. 'You convinced everyone.'

'Except you.'

He approached her again, stroking his hand down one of her slim arms. 'I'm the one who's spent the most time with you. I was drawn to you. You intrigued me.' He captured a handful of her hair and ran it through his fingertips and added, 'You were a beguiling mix of feisty and shy. The stuff I'd been told about you didn't add up, but it wasn't until I did a bit of research after the wedding was called off that I put all the pieces of the puzzle together.'

'What did you find? I asked Elodie to keep quiet about having a twin. I never wanted the fame she's sought since she was a kid. I hate being in the spotlight. I hate being compared to her and found lacking. I've had nightmares for years of people mistaking her for me and chasing me down the street. I dress simply, I never wear make-up or nail polish. I keep the lowest profile I can. I only did the switch because…well, I was a little tired of my boring life. And I genuinely wanted to help her.'

'There was one photo attached to an article about Lincoln Lancaster's aborted wedding. It wasn't a clear shot of you but I could see the likeness. Your name was there along with the other young women. I'm annoyed at myself for not guessing who you were sooner.'

'I'm glad you didn't.' She threw him a churlish glance. 'It might've caused an even bigger scandal if you'd outed me.'

Mack took her hands in his and gave them a gentle squeeze. 'Why did you do it?'

She gave a shuddering sigh. 'Elodie needed to be somewhere else for an important top-secret meeting. She convinced me to go in her place to the wedding, but she didn't tell me anything about her one-night stand with your brother. I was so shocked when he approached me and was no nasty towards me.'

'I'm sorry about his behaviour.'

'It's okay, I'm quite proud of how I managed it, to tell you the truth.' Elspeth frowned and continued, 'But as much as I wanted to put Fraser in his place, there was Sabine to consider. I know you wanted their wedding to go ahead but I was convinced it would be a disaster if it did.'

'You were right,' Mack said with a heavy

sigh. 'Fraser has some serious growing up to do before he's ready to settle down with anyone.'

'There was another reason I agreed to step into my twin's shoes...' Her gaze came back to his. 'Because of my allergy, I've spent most of my life with my mother hovering anxiously over me in case I ingest a peanut. I only moved out of home a month ago and I'm twenty-eight years old. If I checked my phone right now I swear there will be fifty missed calls or texts from her. I have to turn my phone off most of the time otherwise it drives me crazy. The last time I tried to have a weekend away, she turned up. I was so embarrassed having her fussing over me. I decided switching places with Elodie would be a chance to live a little. To experience things I've only ever dreamt about before.'

'What sort of things?'

Her gaze drifted to his mouth. 'The first and only time I was kissed when I was eighteen, I ended up in hospital with anaphylactic shock.'

It took a moment for Mack to realise the import of her confession. 'You mean you haven't been kissed until now?'

Elspeth gave a self-conscious grimace. 'I know, pathetic, right?'

He took her by the upper arms again. 'It's not pathetic. It's… I'm just gobsmacked that I'm the first person to…' He shook his head as another thought occurred to him. She was so inexperienced. He was the first person to kiss her in a decade. He was shocked and yet strangely touched. Honoured that she had allowed him to be the one to be the first. 'Does that mean you're—'

'A virgin? Yes. That's even more pathetic.'

Mack released her to score a hand through his hair. She was a virgin who had only been kissed once before. How could he think of having a fling with her now? He was used to sleeping with women who were at ease with casual relationships. Sleeping with a sweet, shy virgin was not in his game plan. 'No, it's not pathetic at all. But it changes everything between us.'

Elspeth looked at him in alarm. 'What do you mean?'

He waved a hand to encompass their intimate surroundings. 'We'll stay the night here because it'll soon be too dark to go back to the castle but we won't be sleeping together.'

'I see…' Her expression became masklike but he could sense the disappointment in her. The same disappointment he was experiencing. A bitter disappointment that was hard to swallow. 'Can I ask why?'

'For God's sake, Elspeth. You're a virgin and I'm a freaking playboy, that's why.'

She held his gaze with straight-shouldered pride. 'I hardly see how that's a problem. If anything, surely it would be an advantage? You know what to do and can help me.'

Mack rubbed a hand down his face, the sound of his palm raking across his stubble loud in the silence. 'It's not going to happen. I'm not the right person for you.'

'I'm not asking for a commitment, Mack. I just want to experience sex with someone I desire. It can be just the once. I just want to lose my virginity to someone who will treat me with respect. I know you will do that.'

Mack let out a swear word in Gaelic. 'I don't want to talk about it any more.' He stepped back to the table where he had left the box of food. 'We're going to have a drink and a light supper and go to bed. Alone.'

Her gaze drifted to the queen-sized bed through the open door of the bedroom off the living area. 'But there's only one bed.'

'I'll make do on the sofa.' His back began to ache at the thought. And not just his back but other parts of his anatomy that would have preferred sharing that bed with Elspeth.

But how could he do such a thing? She was so innocent, so inexperienced and he had no right to be thinking of taking her in his arms. She was off limits. He had to be strong, in control of his desires, to be honourable and steadfast. He could do that, of course he could. He would have to.

'It won't be very comfortable for you. I'm not as tall—maybe I should sleep there instead.'

Mack shook his head. 'No. You have the bed. I insist.'

'But—'

'No arguments.' He injected his tone with a note of intractability, more for his own benefit than hers. He had to be strong. He had to ignore the chemistry that filled the crofter's hut with unbearable tension. He had to ignore the throbbing need in his body. He had to be out of his mind to even contemplate sleeping with her now he knew about her inexperience.

'Fine. We'll do it your way.' Elspeth swung away and stalked off to the bathroom, clicking the door shut behind her.

Mack let out a ragged sigh and stared at the bottle of champagne in his hand. He had never felt less like celebrating.

# CHAPTER SEVEN

ELSPETH STARED AT her reflection in the bathroom mirror, wishing she hadn't told Mack
the truth. But how could she have slept with
him as her sister? It would be taking the
charade way too far. She hadn't been able
to go any further without him knowing the
truth. But now he knew who she was, he was
pulling away. Was that because she wasn't
enough on her own? That the layer of confidence she'd adopted while pretending to
be her twin had been the allure—the only
thing about her he had found irresistible?
She wasn't enough as herself, but then, she
never had been. She had always been lesser
than her outgoing, talented twin. She had always compared herself to Elodie and felt she
didn't measure up. Not just because of her
allergy, which had limited her life so much,
but because she lacked her twin's assertive-

ness, her audacity and energetic enthusiasm for adventure.

So where did that leave her now?

It left her feeling ashamed and alone and frustrated. Frustrated physically, because Mack's kiss had awoken her flesh and made her hungry for more of his touch. She lifted her fingers to her lips, tracing where his lips had pressed so firmly, so urgently. Her cheeks were still flushed, her body still throbbing with a low, deep, dragging ache.

Her hand fell away from her lips and she released a ragged sigh. How was she going to get a wink of sleep knowing he was only a few feet away, scrunched up on the sofa?

Elspeth came out of the bathroom after freshening up to find Mack had left the crofter's hut, presumably to give her some privacy. Unlike the castle, the walls here were thin, the rooms small, which would have made it the perfect love-tryst location.

*Love?*

She frowned at the word her brain had sourced at random. No, this wasn't love. This was lust. She was experiencing her first full-on body crush. Yes, there were lots of things about Mack besides his body she found enormously attractive. He had known who she was and had brought her up here to keep her away from the press. It was a kind and thoughtful gesture, but it didn't mean she had to fall in love with him because of it. No, she was attracted to him physically.

But then, who wouldn't be? He had drive and ambition in spades, a strong work ethic and he genuinely cared about doing the right thing by people. Which was why he was refusing to sleep with her. Was it because he was worried she would read more into the encounter than was warranted? That he had somehow assumed she would fall instantly in love with him and complicate things for him? She might be a little inexperienced in the ways of the world, but she wasn't a fool. She could handle a sensual encounter without losing her heart to him. One night with him would have been a perfect solution for her. A way of losing her virginity with a man she liked and respected and one who liked and respected her. Why wouldn't he accept the invitation? Was it because he didn't think she could handle a casual hook-up?

Elspeth sat on the sofa and cuddled a scatter cushion against her chest. She hadn't considered herself the casual-dating type. In spite of her sheltered background, she had quietly dreamed of one day finding the right person to settle down with and make a family. But the older she got, the more remote the possibility had become. Who would want her with her faulty immune system? What if she gave one of her children her allergy? There would be a lifetime of worry for her and her partner, not to mention her child. And then her mother would have double the worry. It was easier not to hanker after things other people took for granted. Easier to settle for less than to crave more and be disappointed. And wouldn't she be craving more than she could have by wanting more time with Mack? Wouldn't she be setting herself up for bitter disappointment? For Mack was not the settling-down type. He had stated it baldly—he was a hardened playboy. A man who moved from casual lover to casual lover without long-term commitment on the agenda.

The door opened behind her and Elspeth turned to see Mack coming in with some blocks of peat for the fire. The late summer twilight had brought with it a cool change, the wind was whistling outside in an eerie tone that sounded almost ghostly, ethereal.

'I think we might get a storm in a bit,' Mack said, bending down to attend to the fire.

Elspeth put the scatter cushion to one side

and got off the sofa to peer out of the nearest window. She suppressed a tiny shudder. Storm clouds were gathering, the sky so ominously broody it made the back of her neck prickle. 'It certainly looks a bit wild out there...'

Mack must have sensed something in her tone, for he turned from his kneeling position in front of the fire to look at her over his shoulder. 'You don't like storms?'

She grimaced and wrapped her arms across her middle. 'Not much.'

He closed the firebox and straightened, dusting off his hands on his jeans. 'This hut has withstood plenty of savage storms, so you'll be safe here.'

'What if I don't want to be safe?' She must have been playing her twin too long for the words just popped out as if she had oodles of natural confidence. She was taking a gamble, stepping way outside her comfort zone, terrified he would reject her hands down, but she wouldn't be able to forgive herself if she didn't make the most of this opportunity.

She was alone with him, totally alone and might never have the chance again.

Why shouldn't she be bold and brazen about what she wanted?

Mack rubbed a hand down his face. 'Elspeth. We've already had this conversation.'

'No, Mack. A conversation is where two people express their opinions and listen to each other, each taking on board what the other says.' Elspeth approached him, stopping within touching distance. 'You told me what you wanted without really listening to what I wanted.'

His eyes locked with hers. 'What do you want?'

Elspeth closed the distance between them, sliding her hands up the hard wall of his chest. He sucked in a breath, his body jolting as if touched by a live wire. The same electricity that fired through her own acutely aware flesh. 'I think you know what I want. It's what you want too.'

Mack placed his hands on her hips and brought her flush against his hardened body. 'You don't strike me as the casual-lover type. And that's all I can be right now.'

Elspeth snaked her arms around his neck, tangling her fingers in his windswept hair. He smelt of the outdoors—fresh, wild, untamed. She lowered her gaze to his grimly set mouth. 'What if that was all I wanted right now? A casual lover?'

He tipped up her chin with one of his

hands, his gaze searching. 'Are you sure about this? You might regret it in the morning.'

Elspeth leaned into his rock-hard body, her feminine flesh tingling with anticipation. 'I promise I won't regret it. I want to make love with you. I want it so much I can hardly believe I'm saying it. For all these years, I've ignored the needs of my body. It's like it's been asleep until I met you. Now, all I can think about is how it will feel to be in your arms.'

Mack framed her face in his hands, his gaze still locked on hers. 'You're making it so hard for me to resist you.' His voice was rough around the edges, his body against hers signalling the struggle he had to maintain control.

She smiled and stroked a finger down the length of his nose. 'Look who's talking. You've been making it impossible to resist you from the moment I met you.'

He gave a low deep groan and covered her mouth with his in a passionate kiss that set her blood racing and her heart pumping. His arms came around her, holding her to his body as if he never wanted to let her go. His tongue slipped between her lips and she was lost to the overwhelming force of desire that swept through her like a fast-running tide. Her lips clung to his, her tongue tangling with his, her need matching his. A ferocious need that threatened to consume her.

Mack kissed his way from her mouth down the side of her neck, his lips and tongue teasing her sensitive flesh into a frenzy of want. She tilted her head to one side, shivering and gasping with delight as his tongue caressed the shell of her ear. 'Your skin is so soft…' he said in a husky voice that was like a caress all of its own. 'So soft and fragrant, I think I'm becoming addicted to it.'

'I think I'm developing my own addiction,' she said, stepping on tiptoe to press a kiss to his lips. 'I can't seem to get enough of your mouth.'

He made another guttural sound and deepened the kiss with a commanding thrust of his tongue, the sensations rioting through her body until she was quaking with need. The kiss went on and on, an exchange of passion that fired every nerve of her body into excitement. Warm humid heat pooled in her core, her lower spine trembled, her breasts tingled, her breathing became laboured.

He raised his mouth from hers, his own breathing heavy, and, kicking open the bedroom door with one foot, he led her to the bed. He ran his hands down the sides of her body, his touch light but electric. 'Are you sure about this? It's not too late to change your mind.'

Elspeth gripped the front of his shirt with both of her hands, her lower body pressed tightly against his. 'I'm not changing my mind. I want you. And from what I can tell, you want me too.'

He gave a wry smile and grasped her hips once more. 'It's not like I can hide it.' He brought his mouth back to hers in a long drugging kiss, his tongue playing with hers in a sexy tango that made her blood sing through her veins. Heat bloomed between her thighs, hot damp primal heat that threatened to engulf her. He began to remove her clothes, slowly, gently, anointing her naked skin with his lips and tongue as he went. He left her in just her underwear, his gaze running over her hungrily. 'Your turn.'

Elspeth worked at his clothes but she was trembling so much with need it became almost beyond her capability. 'How do they make this look so darn easy in the movies?' she said, fumbling with his shirt buttons.

Mack smiled and finished the job for her, hauling the shirt to one side. His chest was broad and toned and lightly dusted with rough hair. He had a light tan and flat dark brown nipples. He kicked off his shoes and pulled off his socks and stood in just his jeans. 'Think you can manage the rest?'

Elspeth disguised a gulp and went for the fastener on his jeans. 'I'll give it a go.' Her fingers tingled as soon as she touched his hard, flat abdomen, heat racing up her arm like a live current. She lowered his zip and ran an exploratory finger across the tented bulge of his arousal. 'Wow, pretty impressive.'

He cupped one side of her face in his hand. 'Don't be nervous. I'll go slowly.'

His gentle tone made it hard for her to keep her emotions out of the situation. 'I'm not nervous. I want you.'

'I want you too.' He spoke the words against her lips, then kissed her deeply again. His hands lowered the straps of her bra, then he unclipped the fastener at the back and it fell away to the floor. He lifted his mouth off hers to gaze at her nakedness, his pupils flaring. 'You're so beautiful.'

'Small, you mean.'

'Beautiful.' He brought his mouth to her right breast, his lips soft and yet like fire on her flesh. His tongue traced around her nipple in a fiery pathway, making her shudder with delight. He took her nipple in his mouth and drew on it gently, the tingling sensation making her toes curl and her spine loosen. He moved to her other breast, exploring it in the same exquisite detail, sending shivers through her body.

His hand moved down to cup her most intimate flesh. The sensation of his warm palm against her, even through the barrier of lace, was nothing short of electrifying. She moved instinctively against his hand, yearning for more contact. He stroked a lazy finger down the seam of her body, a light, teasing touch that sent a shock wave through her. The come-and-play-with-me motion of his finger created a firestorm in her flesh and she groaned out loud.

'More…oh, please, more…'

Mack peeled away her knickers and she stepped out of them. She would have over-balanced if he hadn't had hold of her. His eyes were dark and lustrous with want and he drank his fill of her, his breathing rate escalating. 'I can't take my eyes off you.'

'As long as your hands are on me as well, I don't mind what you do with your eyes.' Elspeth pressed a hot kiss to his mouth, pushing herself against him, aching for him in a way she hadn't thought possible. A burning ache that heated her flesh to boiling point. He returned the kiss with a deep groan, his lips and tongue wreaking further havoc on her already dazzled senses.

She was impatient to touch him skin on skin and so, with a boldness she hadn't thought she possessed, she peeled his underwear from his lean hips. She touched him and was rewarded with a deep groan of pleasure that seemed to come right from the centre of his body. It emboldened her to be more daring. She stroked his powerful length, a vicarious thrill of pleasure passing through her own body at the feel of him under the pads of her fingers. He was velvet-wrapped steel, potent and yet strangely vulnerable. She wrapped her fingers around him and squeezed and he sucked in a harsh-sounding breath, a shudder of pleasure visibly rippling through him.

'You're a natural at this,' he said.

'I don't know about that… I'm just feeling my way here.'

'Feel away.'

Elspeth ran her thumb over the head of his erection where some pre-ejaculatory fluid had formed. 'You really do want me, don't you?' Her voice came out in breathless wonder.

'Like I said, I can't hide it.' He pressed her

down on the bed, stopping only long enough before joining her to get a condom. He applied it with a complete lack of self-consciousness and she wondered if he had lost count of the times he had performed the task with other lovers. She was annoyed with herself for thinking about his life as a playboy. What did she care about any of that? He was here with her at this moment, not with anyone else. That was all that mattered.

He came down beside her on the bed and stroked his hand down from her waist to her thigh and back again. 'Are you still okay with this? We can stop at any point.'

Elspeth traced around his sculptured mouth with a slow-moving finger. 'I'm okay. I want this. I want you. This is what I believe is called enthusiastic consent.'

'I wouldn't settle for anything less.' His tone had a note of gravity in it that assured her of his nobleness all over again. Playboy he might be, but he wasn't the sort of man who felt entitled to a woman's body. He was respectful and considerate and Elspeth was glad beyond measure that he was going to be her first lover.

'I know that,' she said, running her finger across his fuller lower lip. 'That's why you're the perfect person to coach me.'

He captured her hand and pressed a kiss to the end of her finger, his gaze holding hers in an intimate lock that sent a frisson through her body. 'I don't want to hurt you.' His voice was low and husky.

'You won't.'

'Sometimes the first time can be painful for some women.'

'How many virgins have you slept with?'

'None.'

Elspeth raised her eyebrows. 'Really?'

He caressed the curve of her cheek with the back and forth movement of his thumb. 'You're the first.'

A thought suddenly occurred to her. 'Are *you* nervous?'

He grimaced, then squeezed her hand and planted another kiss on her fingertip. 'I'm nervous about you placing more significance on us making love than what's necessary.'

Elspeth gave him a playful punch on the arm, not all that surprised his muscles were as hard as stone. 'Will you stop trying to make me out as some sort of romance tragic who can't tell the difference between casual and committed sex? I have my feet planted firmly on the ground, although not right at this moment because I'm lying here with you—which feels amazing, by the way.' She ran her finger down his sternum to his belly button and back up again. 'I'm not going to beg you to marry me, Mack. After my twin's and Sabine's cancelled weddings, I'm starting to think weddings and me are a terrible combination.'

He gave a crooked smile and captured her hand once more, holding it against the throbbing heat of his body. 'So, we're clear on the rules, then there's nothing to stop me doing this.' He brought his mouth down to hers in a blisteringly hot kiss that made her skin tingle all over. He lifted his mouth from hers and continued, 'Or this.' He placed his lips on her breast, stroking his tongue around her nipple until her back arched off the bed.

Elspeth gasped and moved closer to the heat of his body, searching for him instinctively, aching for him with a primal ache that was uncontrollable. He moved down her body with a series of kisses that made her nerves twitch with need. He finally came to the heart of her femininity, the warm moist cave of her body that was preparing in secret for his possession. He brought his mouth to her folds, separating her with his tongue, his lips playing with her sensitised flesh, sending waves of tingling pleasure through her body. Delicious tension began to build in her swollen tissues, tension that grew to a crescendo. A storm of sensation that threatened to erupt at any moment. His tongue flicked against her in a repetitive motion, fast and yet gentle flickers that triggered an explosion in her flesh. Her back arched, her legs stiffened, her toes curled as an orgasm rippled through her in giant waves. It went on and on, sending bright starbursts off behind her tightly closed eyes. Her body thrashed beneath the ministrations of his clever mouth, the sensations carrying her away to a place where all conscious thought was pushed aside.

Mack stroked the length of her thigh in the aftermath, his gaze warm and tender. 'It gets better.'

Elspeth let out a fluttering breath. 'You have to be joking. How could anything be better than that?'

He planted a soft kiss on her mouth, one of his hands cupping her breast. 'I'll show you.'

'I can hardly wait.'

He smiled a sexy smile that made her toes curl all over again. 'I won't make you wait too long.'

Elspeth kissed him back. 'You'd better not or I won't be answerable for the consequences.'

'Should I be afraid?' Mack gave her a teasing look, his eyes twinkling.

'Very.' She lifted her face for his kiss, losing herself in the sheer magic of the erotic choreography of their lips and tongue.

He moved over her, separating her legs with a gentle placement of his hand on her thigh, his strong body positioned so as not to crush her with his weight. She clasped him tightly to her, wanting more contact, wanting the closest contact of all. He nudged her entrance, testing her readiness, his gentle sounds of encouragement helping her to relax. He slid in a small distance, waiting for her to get used to him, one of his hands softly stroking her face.

'Are you okay?' His eyes were dark, his tone gentle, his touch magical.

'I'm fine. You feel…amazing…' She found herself whispering the words in wonder. Her body was so ready for him, so hungry it welcomed him without a twinge of discomfort.

'So do you.' He kissed her on the lips and went a little deeper, his body thick and strong. He began slowly thrusting, allowing her time to catch the rhythm of his body within hers. Her flesh tightened around him, accepting him, wanting him, needing him as she needed air to breathe. The pleasurable sensations began to build within her core, the tension ramping up until she was desperate to fly free once more. But she wasn't quite able to get there with just the movements of his body within her. She arched her spine, needing more friction at the heart of her flesh but not sure how to get it.

Mack slipped his hand down between their bodies, touching her swollen tenderness with expert precision, the coaxing movement of his fingers against her sending her into the stratosphere within a heartbeat. The orgasm rocked through her like a storm, tossing her about in a sea of sensation that left no part of her unaffected. Her body tingled from head to foot, all her nerves and tissues in rapturous pleasure unlike anything she could have ever imagined. The ripples continued in pulsing waves that triggered his own release. Elspeth held him as his body shuddered with the power of it, his final deep thrusts sending another wave of pleasure through her. It shocked her a little to think she had given him such a thunderous release. She, who had had no experience of sex until now. She hadn't considered herself a sensual person at all and yet here she was lying in Mack's arms in the aftermath of a blissful encounter. Who knew her body could be so in tune with his?

Or maybe it was always like that for him. All of his lovers had a good time in his arms.

She was nothing special. How could she be? They were keeping their relationship casual.

But wouldn't it be wonderful to be his special someone? The person he chose to be with for longer than a night or two. Elspeth tried not to allow her mind to wander down that path…the path of happy ever after. But how could she not after experiencing such tenderness, such passion and excitement in his arms?

# CHAPTER EIGHT

MACK LEANED ON one elbow to look down at her, his other hand brushing the hair back from her forehead, momentarily lost for words. Her eyes were bright and luminous, her lips plump and swollen from his kisses, her slim legs still entwined with his. His body hummed with the aftershocks of pleasure—stunning, earth-shattering pleasure—that had taken him completely by surprise. The physical connection between them surpassed that of his other encounters but he wasn't too keen on examining why. It raised a red flag in his head. Questioning why this encounter was so unique was a no-go zone. It had to be. He only did casual relationships. He didn't commit. He didn't make promises. He didn't offer what he couldn't give.

Elspeth brought her hand up to his face, her palm soft as a cloud against his cheek.

'Thank you.' Her voice was barely above a whisper and contained a note of wonder.

Mack captured her hand and kissed each of her fingertips, his eyes holding hers. 'I should be the one thanking you.' He realised with a jolt how honoured he felt to be her first lover. Was that why their encounter had been so special? So off the charts in sensuality and connection?

'For what?'

'For choosing me to be your first lover.'

Her gaze lowered to his mouth for a moment, her cheeks going a faint shade of pink. 'I'm glad it was you. I can't imagine making love with anyone else.'

The bright red flag popped up in his head again. Mack was finding it hard to imagine making love with anyone else too. Who else would respond to him with such passionate intensity? With such sweet and trusting generosity? Her body had felt like an extension of his own, it worked with his in perfect tandem, producing a stunning eruption of pleasure from which he was yet to recover. He dropped a kiss to her mouth and then carefully eased away, making a business of disposing of the condom, when really what he wanted to dispose of were his wayward thoughts. Thoughts of offering her a relationship, a short-term fling where they could explore the passion that had flared between them from the moment they met. Would that be crossing a line? Taking things further than what was wise?

He wanted her.

She wanted him.

What else mattered for now?

Mack came back to where Elspeth was lying on the bed. He gazed down at her nakedness with fire burning with molten heat in his blood. He bent down on one knee, and placing his hands either side of her head, leaned over her to press a lingering kiss to her mouth. He lifted his mouth off hers. 'I should be offering you food but I keep wanting to kiss you.'

'I'm not hungry for food.' She touched one of her fingers against his lips. 'I'm hungry for you.'

He took her hand and gave it a gentle squeeze. 'Elspeth…' He took a deep breath, still trying to get his head around what he was about to say. He didn't want this to be a one-nighter like so many of his other casual encounters. The passion they had shared put it in an entirely different category. But what could he offer that wouldn't compromise his strict relationship rules? He wasn't interested in settling down. He wasn't interested in anything permanent.

But he was interested in exploring more of the sensual energy that had erupted with such stunning force between them.

Elspeth pulled her hand away and sat upright, covering her nakedness with the bed throw rug as if suddenly conscious of her lack of clothing. 'Is this the part where you lecture me about how you only do casual relationships? That what happened between us just now is a one-off and won't be repeated?'

There was a long beat of silence. It was as if the crofter's hut had taken a deep breath, not even a creak of old timber or the rattle of a windowpane daring to break the intense silence. Even the wild wind outside seemed to have abated to a breathless, barely audible whisper.

Mack sat on the bed beside her, reaching for one of her hands. 'Hey.' He enveloped her small hand within his, a little tingle of pleasure running through him at the contact. 'Look at me.'

Elspeth turned her head to look at him, her teeth momentarily sinking into her bottom lip. 'I know what you're going to say…' There was a hint of bleak resignation in her tone that unexpectedly tugged on his heart-strings.

He bumped up her chin with his index finger. 'Actually, I don't think you do.'

Her gaze shimmered and a look of puzzlement crept over her face. 'What are you going to say, then?'

Mack gave a slow smile and stroked a lazy finger down the slope of her cheek. 'I don't want this to be a one-off. I want you to come away with me for a few days. I have a villa in the South of France—we can have a short holiday together. By the time we get back, the press will have forgotten all about Fraser's wedding being cancelled. Then you can go back to your life, I can go back to mine.'

Her smooth brow furrowed and her eyes moved back and forth between his as if searching for something. 'Are you sure?'

Mack was sure of one thing and one thing only. He wanted her. 'I wouldn't ask you if I wasn't.'

A smile broke over her features and something in his chest flipped open. 'I would love to come.'

He gave her a smouldering look. 'We'll pack up in the morning. But for now, I have something to do.'

'I wonder what that could be.' Her tone was playful, her eyes bright and shining.

'Guess.' And he lowered his mouth to hers.

Elspeth woke during the night to find herself spooned by Mack's firm warm body, the coarse hair of his forearms tickling the sensitive skin underneath her breasts. It had been hours since they had made love for the second time, but her body was still humming with delicious aftershocks. Every time she thought of his powerful body entering her, a soft flutter passed through her lower body—a tiny, secretive frisson of remembered pleasure.

Mack let out a long, deep sigh and gathered her closer, her bottom coming into contact with the hard ridge of his growing erection. 'What are you doing awake at this hour?' His voice had a playfully gruff edge. He began to nuzzle the side of her face, the prickly regrowth on his jaw sending hot tingles down her spine.

Elspeth turned in his arms and slid one of her feet down his hair-roughened calf. 'I could ask the same of you.'

He rolled her beneath him, his gaze holding hers in a tender lock. 'It's too soon to make love again. I don't want you to get sore. You're new to this.'

'You have to stop treating me like I'm made of glass. I can handle anything you do to me.' A doubt popped up its head. *Anything?* Well, maybe not quite anything. The one thing she didn't want from him was a broken heart.

But she could keep her feelings out of this, after all, other people did.

Her twin did.

Why couldn't she?

Mack stroked his thumb over her lower lip in a fainéant movement. 'The last thing I want to do is hurt you.' His voice was low and gravel-rough, his expression etched in lines of concern.

Elspeth had a feeling he wasn't talking about physical hurt. 'I'm a big girl, Mack. I know how to take care of myself.'

He gave a lopsided smile and stroked her lower lip again. 'As long as we're both clear on the rules.'

She tiptoed her fingers all the way down his sternum and his taut and ripped-with-muscle abdomen. 'I think you need the rules for you, not for me.' She challenged him with her gaze and added, 'Am I right?' Her hand was poised just above the hot hard heat of his length.

He gave a shudder and groaned deep in his throat. 'There should be a rule against you looking so damn sexy first thing in the morning.'

She stroked her hand over his thickened erection. 'I'm sure you could resist me if you wanted to.'

His eyes darkened to gunmetal grey. 'I can't resist you. Not right now.' His mouth came down firmly on hers, sweeping her away on a tide of blissful longing, one she wondered if she would ever stop craving in spite of the rules.

It was late the following afternoon by the time they arrived at Mack's villa in the quaint medieval village of Lagrasse in the Occitanie region in the South of France. The villa was a large stone building that overlooked the River Orbieu and it had a wonderful view of the abbey that the village was subsequently built around.

Mack helped Elspeth out of the car. 'What do you think so far?' he asked.

Elspeth did a complete circle, taking in the breathtaking view. The warm summer late afternoon breeze caressed her face, the smell of flowers redolent in the air. 'It's gorgeous, Mack. I didn't even know this village existed before you brought me here. It's like stepping back in time.'

He looped an arm around her waist, leading her to the front door. 'It's reputed to be one of the most beautiful villages in the South of France. The wine from this region is spectacular.'

She playfully shoulder-bumped him. 'Did someone mention wine?'

He grinned and leaned down to plant a kiss on her lips. 'Am I corrupting you?'

Elspeth smiled back. 'Yes, but I'm enjoying every minute of it. How long have you had this place?'

'A couple of years now,' Mack said, and unlocked the door and turned off an alarm with a fob on the keyring. 'I have a housekeeper who checks on things and a gardener-cum-maintenance-man. They see to things when I can't be here as much as I'd like.' He pushed the door open for her and waved her inside.

Elspeth stepped over the threshold and looked around in amazement. The villa was tastefully decorated in a French Provincial style with lots of white and grey and exposed woodwork. It didn't have the grand ostentatiousness of Mack's Scottish estate and she wondered if that was why he liked it. She turned to face him. 'How often do you come here?'

'Four or five times a year, often for only short visits, unfortunately. I have a lot of other business to see to at home.'

'Do you enjoy it? Your business interests, I mean?'

He closed the solid front door, his expression rueful. 'Not always. I inherited a lot of debt when my father died. I had no choice but to put my own career aspirations on hold and do what had to be done. It's taken a long time to get back in the black. Once you've stared down bankruptcy, it's hard to truly relax, no matter how much money you make. I have a lot of people depending on me.' He blew out a sigh and continued, 'And no doubt Fraser will be one of them now his dream job has been taken away.'

Elspeth placed a hand on his arm. 'I'm sorry things have been so difficult for you. You've given up so much for your family.'

He flicked her cheek with a gentle finger. 'Stop apologising. I'm happy enough.'

But was he? Did worldly possessions and plenty of money in the bank give him the fulfilment most people craved? He struck her as a loner, a man who stood apart from others. He kept his relationships short and casual. The only commitment he was prepared to make was to his career. A career he hadn't even chosen for himself but had inherited due to tragic circumstances.

'What did you want to do?' Elspeth asked after a moment. 'I mean, career wise?'

His smile was crooked. 'Nothing that would've made me anywhere near the money I've made. Come. Let me show you around before I bring in our luggage.'

Elspeth got the feeling he wasn't comfortable talking about that aspect of his life. The hopes and dreams he had left behind in order to protect his family's assets. It would have taken great courage and commitment to pull his family's finances out of the red. He had done it and done it brilliantly, but at what cost to himself?

After Mack gave her a quick tour of the villa, Elspeth wandered around on her own while he brought in their luggage. She was eager to explore all of the quaint rooms in more detail but even more eager to wander about the garden. She walked out of the kitchen door to a paved courtyard where pots of fresh herbs grew as well as a long row of purple lavender. Bees were busily taking the pollen from the lavender heads; numerous small birds were twittering in the trees and nearby shrubbery. It was easy to see why Mack loved coming here. The setting was so serene and restful, especially when the abbey's bells began to toll in the distance. She closed her eyes and listened to the rhythmic peels of the ancient bells, a mantle of peace settling over her.

Elspeth turned at the sound of a footfall to see Mack coming out of the villa carrying a bottle of champagne and two glasses. 'You really know the way to a girl's heart.' She could have bitten her tongue off for the vocal slip. He wasn't after her heart. He wanted no emotional commitment from her. All he wanted was a fling and she was fine with that because she had to be.

There was no other choice.

'When in France, do as the French do,' he said with a smile. He popped the cork and poured the bubbles into the two glasses and then handed her one. *'Á votre santé.'* His perfect French accent almost made her swoon. Was there no end to this man's heart-stopping charms?

Elspeth returned the toast in French. *'Á votre santé.'* The champagne was exquisite, the bubbles exploding in her mouth and tantalising her taste buds. She couldn't help thinking it was going to be hard to go back to drinking cheap sparkling wine once their fling was over. Her old life seemed so staid and boring and uneventful after just a couple of days in Mack MacDiarmid's company.

'What are you thinking?' Mack asked.

Elspeth gave him a self-conscious smile. 'I was thinking how hard it's going to be for me to go back to my boring life after this.'

A small frown pulled at his forehead. He put his champagne down. 'Why do you think your life is boring?'

She gave a one-shoulder shrug. 'Because it is. I work. I eat, I sleep. Alone.'

'You have friends though, don't you?'

'Yes, but I don't socialise much.' Elspeth plucked one of the lavender stalks off and twirled it beneath her nose.

'Because of your allergy?'

She glanced at him to find him watching her steadily. 'Not just because of that. My twin is the social butterfly, not me. I'm happy in my own company. As long as I have a good book, I'm content.'

Mack came closer and lifted her chin so her gaze met his. 'Have you always lived in Elodie's shadow?'

Elspeth let the lavender stalk drop to the ground. 'Mostly. She's way more outgoing than me. I can't compete so I don't bother trying.' She twisted her mouth and added, 'She's everything I'm not.'

Mack stroked her chin with the pad of his thumb. 'But you're you. And that's all you ever need to be.' He bent his head and lowered his mouth to hers in a kiss that stirred a deep longing in her flesh and in her heart. A longing for more than physical connection.

A forbidden longing.

He lifted his mouth off hers and stroked her chin once more. 'Have you ever switched places with her before?'

Elspeth put her champagne glass down, deciding that the delicious champagne was messing with her head and her heart. 'A few times when we were kids.' She gave a little half-laugh and continued, 'Our mother was never fooled but our father could never tell us apart. Not even when he lived with us.'

'Your parents are no longer together?'

'No. They divorced when we were five. We'd stopped being cute by then, so he decided to move on. He had a second family with another woman. A boy and a girl, neither of whom have allergies, for which he is mightily relieved.'

Mack frowned so deeply it formed a trench between his eyes. 'You think your allergy had something to do with your parents' divorcing?'

Elspeth wished she'd kept her wayward mouth shut. What was it with her? A mouthful or two of champagne and she was spilling all. Spilling things she had told no one, apart from her twin, before. 'It contributed, certainly. I had almost lost my life three or four times by then. My father doesn't handle stress too well.'

'It's not your fault he didn't have the maturity to handle a sick child. That's on him, not you.'

'I know but it can't have been easy, you know? My mum was a worrier at the best of times. My allergy diagnosis turned her into a nervous wreck. She has no life apart from me.' She grimaced and turned to pick up her champagne again, staring down at the vertical necklaces of bubbles rising. 'I sometimes feel like I ruined her life.'

His hands came down on the tops of her shoulders from behind. 'Don't say that. I'm sure she doesn't think that at all.' His voice was deep and low and husky.

Elspeth leaned back against him, drawn to him as an iron filing was drawn to a magnet. 'You have to stop giving me champagne.'

'Why?'

She turned in the circle of his arms and handed him her glass. 'Because I keep telling you things I've never told anyone else before.'

He put her glass to one side. 'Why is that a problem?'

Elspeth gave a rueful smile. 'Because we're practically strangers, that's why.'

He picked up a loose strand of her hair and tucked it behind her ear, his touch so gentle it made her heart tighten. 'You don't feel like a stranger to me.' His voice was still as rough as the pockmarked flagstones beneath their feet. 'And if it's any comfort to you, I've shared things with you I haven't shared with anyone else.'

Elspeth looked into his grey-blue eyes, struck by how dark and lustrous they were. 'Really?'

His smile was crooked. 'You have a strange effect on me, Elspeth Campbell.'

She moved closer, winding her arms around his neck so her lower body was flush with his. 'So I can tell. Thing is, what are we going to do about it?'

'This,' he said and covered her mouth with his.

Mack wondered if he would ever get tired of kissing her soft mouth. The sweet taste of her filled his senses, dazzled his senses into overload. He was supposed to be keeping her at arm's length but every time he was near her, he wanted her with an ever more pounding ache. It was like a fever in his blood—a virulent fever that had no other antidote but her.

Her body's response to him fuelled his desire. Making him burn, boil and blister with the need to get as close as humanly possible. He dragged his hungry mouth off hers only long enough to groan, 'I want you.'

'I want you too.' Her voice was whisper-soft, her beautiful blue eyes shining with desire. The same desire he could feel pummelling through his body. A desire that begged, pleaded, roared to be assuaged as soon as possible.

Mack couldn't wait for her to walk inside with him. He scooped her up in his arms and carried her indoors.

'What are you doing?' she squeaked. 'You'll do your back in.'

'I like holding you in my arms.'

'I like being held by you but that doesn't mean I can't walk on my own.'

'Indulge me. I've never carried a woman up three flights of stairs before. It'll be good for me.'

She laughed and linked her arms around his neck. 'Crazy man. You're a glutton for punishment.'

Glutton was right. Mack was hungry for her in a way he had not been for anyone else. It shocked him how much he wanted her. How could he have thought he could resist her? How could he have thought one night was going to quell the hot tight ache of his flesh? Why else had he brought her away to France? He wanted more time with her— time to explore the explosive chemistry that flared between them. The chemistry he had felt the first time he had been in the same room as her.

Was it her inexperience that had so impacted him? That she had gifted him herself in such a trusting way? How could he not be honoured and touched by her trust in him? How could he not be affected by their mutual desire? He couldn't explain the deep connection he felt with her. It was beyond anything he had experienced before.

And all he knew was, he wanted to experience it again. And again. With her.

Only with her.

# CHAPTER NINE

ELSPETH SENSED THE urgency in him all the way to his bedroom. She could feel it in the bunched muscles of his arms as he carried her, she could feel it in the blisteringly hot kisses he planted on her lips along the way, she could feel it in the charged atmosphere. An electric charge that threatened to combust at any moment. Her own body was on fire with need—a smouldering simmering need that heated her inner core to boiling.

Mack shouldered open the master-suite door like a hero from an old Hollywood movie. Her heart rate spiked, her pulse leapt, her body burned. He laid her on the bed and set to work on her clothes, only stopping long enough to help her with his.

Finally, they were both naked, their limbs tangled, his mouth coming down on hers in a kiss that nearly blew the top of her head off. His tongue slipped between her lips with erotic purpose, sending a wave of raw lust coursing powerfully through her body. Her back arched in delight, her spine loosening vertebra by vertebra, clawing need spiralling through every cell of her flesh.

'I can't get enough of you,' Mack said, bringing his mouth to the sensitive skin of her neck. 'I want to kiss you all over.'

'You only get to kiss me all over if I get to do the same to you. Deal?' Elspeth was constantly amazed at how brazen she was with him. Brazen and bold with no hint of the shyness that had plagued her most of her life. It was as if she was a completely different person when she was with him. A sensual, adventurous person who was not afraid of expressing her primal needs. But then, he was the only man who had ever made her aware of such needs. She had been asleep before she met him. Locked in a sensual coma that one kiss from him had rescued her from with such stunning impact she could never be the same again. She wouldn't be able to go back to being the quiet shy person she used to be. The person who had convinced herself she was satisfied with her lot in life. The person who had given up any hope of having a partner and family. The person who lived in the shadow of her outgoing twin and was resigned about doing so.

That girl was gone.

She had morphed into a woman with sensual needs that could no longer be ignored.

Mack MacDiarmid had changed her. He made her want things she had denied herself for so long. But there was no denying it now. Her need for him was shouting out from every corner of her body, every blood cell throbbed with it, every heartbeat carrying its primal message.

He captured her hand and pressed a warm kiss to the middle of her palm. His eyes held hers in an intimate lock that made her spine loosen even more. 'I don't want you to feel pressured to do anything you're not comfortable doing.'

'Here's the thing...' Elspeth tiptoed her fingers from his lower lip to the base of his chin and back again. 'I'm completely comfortable with you. I want to pleasure you the way you pleasure me.'

His eyes glinted and he pressed another kiss to her palm, his lips making her skin tingle right the way to her core. 'Everything you do pleasures me.' He brought his mouth down to hers in a long kiss that simmered with passion. His tongue began a playful dance with hers, cajoling hers into a duel that made her insides coil tightly with lust. She stroked her hand down his lean jaw, her softer skin catching on his stubble. He groaned and deepened the kiss even further, his breathing becoming as heavy and laboured as hers.

Elspeth ran one of her hands down his muscled shoulders and the long length of his spine. Touching him was such a delight to her, a thrilling delight that filled her with excitement. His body was hard, toned, tanned and powerful and yet he was so gentle and careful with her.

Mack rolled over to his back, taking her with him so she was lying on top of him, her legs splayed either side of his pelvis. Her hair hung in long tresses, dangling over the hard wall of his chest. His hands held her by the hips, his eyes roving over her naked breasts and belly, his pupils flaring, his breathing going up another notch. 'I could look at you all day. Just like this.'

Elspeth leaned down to press a kiss to his mouth. 'I like looking at you too. But maybe later, because I have something I want to do first.' She wriggled down his body until her mouth was close to the potent length of him. He sucked in a harsh-sounding breath, his hands gripping the bedcovers either side of his body.

'Elspeth, you don't have to… Ahh…' The rest of his sentence faded away as Elspeth got to work on him. She used her lips and tongue in ways she hadn't thought she'd ever have the courage or even the desire to do. But it was a form of worship to caress and pleasure him in such a raw and intimate way. She was rewarded by his deep gasping groans and hectic breathing. But before she could tip him over the edge, he grabbed her by the shoulders and pulled her off him.

'I want to be inside you.' His voice was husky with need. 'But I need a condom.' He gently eased her off him to access a condom from the bedside drawer. He put it on and she straddled him again. Seeing him so turgid with need ramped up her own excitement, her body craving his possession as an addict did a forbidden drug. 'This way you can control the depth,' he said, guiding himself into her entrance.

The sensation of him entering her this way took her breath away. Her body gripped him, her intimate muscles welcoming him, pleasure rippling through her as she began to move. He was right—she could control the depth and speed and it gave her shivers to rock with him in such an erotic way. She ached for more friction and discovered that with just a slight tilt of her body she could get it right where she needed it. The sensations trickled through her, slowly at first, then rising to a crescendo. Tension built in the most sensitive part of her, the surrounding nerves on high alert, waiting for the point of no return. And then it came with a rush of feeling that fanned out in pulsing waves from her core to the farther reaches of her body. She shook, she shuddered, she screamed with the cataclysmic force of it.

Within seconds, Mack followed with his own shuddering release. Watching him in his moment of bliss was both thrilling and deeply erotic. His face screwed up tightly in pleasure, he expelled a deep agonised groan, his body bucked and rocked and then finally relaxed.

Elspeth stayed where she was, perched on top of him, his body still encased in hers. She stroked his chest with her hands in slow-motion movements, watching as his breathing gradually slowed down. 'You look like you had a good time.'

He opened one eye and smiled a crooked smile. 'I did. Did you?'

She leaned down to kiss the tip of his strong nose. 'You know I did.'

He placed his hand at the back of her head and kept her mouth pressed to his. His kiss was slow and sensual, a kiss that sent shivers through her flesh and a flicker of hope to her heart. Could he be developing feelings other than lust for her? Their lovemaking was so physically passionate but there was another element to it that made her wonder if he felt an emotional connection as well.

Or was she fooling herself? Perhaps he made exquisite love to all his lovers. Perhaps they too were stunned by his touch, his kisses and his ability to give them mind-blowing pleasure. Was she being a silly little romantic fool to make more of their love-making than what was there? They desired each other, they had indulged that desire and he had made no promises that anything more lasting would come out of it.

But she couldn't help wanting more than a casual fling. Her feelings for him were growing by the second. They weren't something she could control. How could she have thought she could? They just were *there*. Feelings she had never expected to feel for someone so quickly but how could she resist Mack? He had stunned her from the moment she met him. Wasn't that why she had fought to stay in her twin's persona when in his presence? Because he spoke to *her* in a visceral way from day one. She was falling for him as an autumn leaf was programmed to fall from a tree. She couldn't stop it. It was like a force of nature, a primal thing that swept her up in a world of intense sensuality, one she never wanted to leave.

But how could she hope to stay with a man who didn't want anything more than a fling? A man who had never been in love and was convinced he would never fall in love?

Mack broke off the kiss and, after disposing of the condom, began to stroke his hands down her arms from shoulder to wrist, his touch gentle and yet electrifying. He lifted one of his hands to her face, stroking from below her ear to her chin and back again. He didn't say a word but his expression was cast in lines of contemplation, as if he was mulling over things in his mind. There was a small frown between his brows and a faraway look in his eyes.

Elspeth brushed her fingers through his hair in a tender caress. 'What are you thinking?'

He blinked a couple of times and gave a smile that didn't quite make the full distance to his eyes. 'Not much.' He gave her cheek another stroke and then placed his hand on the small of her back. 'I should feed you. Are you hungry?'

'A bit.'

He gently eased away from her and got off the bed, reaching for his underwear and trousers and stepping into them. Elspeth scrambled off the other side of the bed, suddenly feeling shy. 'I think I'll have a shower...'

Mack came over to her and lifted her chin with his index finger, his eyes searching hers. 'I'm glad you came here with me.'

'I'm glad you asked me.'

He smiled and dropped another kiss to her lips. 'I'll rustle us up some food. We can eat out on the terrace.'

'Sounds lovely.'

Elspeth made her way to the bathroom and stood under a refreshing shower, her thoughts tied up in knots. Every time Mack kissed her, every time he made love with her, every time he even looked at her, her heart leapt. Her twin could handle a fling, Elspeth could not. She didn't have the emotional software. It was like running the wrong operating system on a computer—it was incompatible with her nature. She didn't have the emotional armour to keep her feelings out of it. Was it because he was her first lover? Didn't they say no one ever forgot their first lover? Some couldn't forget because the experience wasn't pleasant, others because it was special, a once-in-a-lifetime event that signalled the beginning of sexual activity.

Making love that first time with Mack was unforgettable and each time since, even more so. His touch was imprinted on her flesh, she couldn't imagine wanting anyone else to touch her. She couldn't imagine wanting any other lips to kiss hers, any other arms to hold her close.

And that was a problem because Mack didn't hold his lovers close for long.

Mack organised some food and drink but his mind was still replaying every moment of their recent lovemaking. He'd had plenty of lovers in the past and not one of them had made him feel the way Elspeth did. Her touch unlocked something inside him, opening up possibilities in his head he had never considered before. The possibility of having more than a short-term fling with her. Not anything too serious, of course. There was a boundary line in his head he had no intention of ever stepping over, not even for someone as adorable as Elspeth. But he did want more time with her. How could he have thought a few days would be enough? Normally it would be. He'd be ready to move on and wouldn't have a twinge of conscience about doing so.

The word 'love' wasn't totally foreign to him. He had loved his mother deeply, he had even loved his father, for all his faults. And he loved his brother and only wanted the best for him. He even loved his father's love child, his half-sister, Daisy. He had invested in her life, paying for her education and visiting her and her mother when he could. It was the least he could do after the devastation his father had caused in their lives.

But loving someone in a romantic sense had never been a possibility and he wasn't sure it ever could be. It hadn't even crossed his mind before now. He hadn't allowed it to. But something about Elspeth made him realise he had been short-changing himself in his relationships. He had always held part of himself back. He had engaged physically but not emotionally. Sex was just sex. It was a pleasant experience that had satisfied him physically but left him empty emotionally.

But not with Elspeth.

Something stirred in him every time he was with her. A soft flutter in his chest, like the hard-shelled pupa of a moth or butterfly slowly opening. He wanted more time with her. More time to explore the chemistry they shared but also more time to get to know her. Not to fall in love with her. That wasn't his game plan at all.

Elspeth came wandering into the kitchen with her hair still damp from her shower. Her face was completely bare of make-up and yet she looked as stunningly beautiful as ever. She was wearing a simple sleeveless dress that skimmed her body in all the right places, flowing out in a wide skirt around her ankles. Her feet were bare, which made her seem even more petite next to him. She carried over her shoulder a small bag that he assumed carried her EpiPens and her phone. He could only imagine the background worry she must deal with on a daily basis because of her allergy. He had been extra vigilant over preparing their supper, giving his housekeeper strict instructions to remove all nuts and nut products and to thoroughly clean all surfaces.

'Can I help?' she asked with a smile.

Mack leaned down to press a kiss to her mouth. 'You'll only distract me. Go and take the wine out to the terrace. I'll bring some supper out in a minute.'

She snaked her arms around his waist, her slim body pressing up against his sending fireworks through his blood. He hardened to stone, his need of her rising with every one of his heartbeats. 'I like distracting you.'

Mack liked it too, way too much. 'Wicked little minx.' He gathered her in his arms and lowered his mouth to hers in a deep kiss that made the hairs of the back of his neck stand up. He stroked one of his hands up and down the slender length of her spine, crushing her to him, relishing in the feel of her breasts pressed against his chest. Was there no end to this burning desire he had for her? He wanted her with a hunger that was relentless, all consuming, overwhelming.

She murmured sounds of encouragement and pressed even closer, one of her hands reaching up to play with his hair. Her touch sent shivers rolling down his spine, making him ache to possess her.

But he had to prove to himself he wasn't completely driven by raw desire. He had to prove to himself he could resist her because surely this craziness would soon burn itself out? It *always* did. The first flush of lust would soon fade to the point where he couldn't wait to get away. To move on to other more exciting pastures. He never wanted someone longer than a few days. He didn't want the complication of a long-term relationship. He didn't seek it, he didn't encourage it, he didn't allow it.

And yet…and yet…something kept tugging at him deep inside, a vague sense that he was somehow robbing himself by keeping things short and shallow. Mostly because it was impossible to be shallow with Elspeth. She was sweet and caring, with deep layers of intelligence he was only beginning to discover. She had deep insights about life in spite of her sheltered existence. A wise perspective on people and relationships that he admired.

Mack gave her bottom a playful pat and lifted his mouth off hers. 'Hold that thought. Supper first.'

Elspeth gave a mock pout. 'Spoilsport.'

Mack couldn't resist planting one more kiss to her lips because her mouth was the most kissable he had ever come across. 'Off you go before I change my mind.'

She stroked a soft hand down the line of his jaw, her gaze suddenly uncomfortably direct. 'Does that ever happen? You changing your mind?'

Mack released her with a tight smile. 'Not

often. And certainly not when emotions are involved.'

'Do you ever allow them to be involved?'

'No.'

She smiled back and picked up the tray off the bench that had a bottle of local wine and two glasses on it. 'That's what I thought.' But something about her tone made him wonder if she was disappointed with his answer.

# CHAPTER TEN

ELSPETH TOOK THE tray out to the terrace where the rising moon was casting a silvery glow across the landscape. An owl hooted its melancholy notes from a tree nearby, frogs started a throbbing chorus from the pond in the garden. The night air was sweet and fragrant with the scent of jasmine and lavender and some other exotic perfume she couldn't identify.

She placed the tray on the wrought-iron table setting and poured herself a glass of the crisp white wine. She took it with her to the edge of the terrace, where a stone balustrade separated the area from the tiered garden below. She took a sip of the wine, letting her tongue savour the taste for a moment, but even top-shelf wine couldn't remove the taste of Mack from her mouth. He was proving every bit as addictive as the wine and she wondered how she was going to deal with the end of their fling. He hadn't put a definitive timeline on it. They were here in the South of France for a few days. Did that mean their fling would end once they returned to the UK?

'Here we go.' Mack joined her on the terrace with a tray with a wheel of camembert cheese and fruit, as well as a fresh baguette. He put the tray down and handed her a side plate and a napkin. 'Help yourself.'

Elspeth was surprised to find she was starving and came back to the table to load up her plate. She sat down and waited for him to join her. He put a small portion of cheese and fruit on his own plate and poured himself half a glass of wine and took the seat opposite her. *'Bon appetit.'*

'Did you learn French at school?' she asked.

'Yes. But we also used to travel to France for summer holidays before my father died.' A shadow passed over his face and he continued, 'Those were happy times.' His lips twisted. 'After he died, it made me question everything about our lives. He always seemed happy enough with my mother and she was certainly happy with him. He was an involved father, or as much as he could be when he was home. He travelled a lot for business, or so he said.'

'What triggered the mental-health crisis that led to his suicide?'

Mack put his glass down on the table with a thud, his expression taut. 'My mother found out he had a mistress and a love child in another city. He'd been with her for five years. He juggled both families and his business all that time but, of course, it was never going to end well. He ran into money troubles, big troubles, and then it all came crashing down. His two lives collided.'

'Oh…how awful that must have been for your mum. But also for his lover. What happened to her and the child? They too must have been distraught when he died.'

Mack picked up his wine glass again and swirled the contents into a tiny whirlpool, his expression still set in shadowed lines. 'They were, especially Daisy, my half-sister. She was only four at the time. It was harrowing to see her and her mother at his funeral.' His throat moved up and down and he continued, 'I'll never forget the sound of them sobbing. It was so…so raw… My mother didn't want them there but I insisted.' His lips twisted again. 'I'm not sure I did the right thing by being so adamant about it. My mother was furious with me for months over it. But Daisy was just a little kid who had just lost her father. She needed closure. So did her mother, Clara.'

Elspeth leaned forward and reached for his free hand and gave it a gentle squeeze. 'It was so good of you to insist on them being there. Of course it would have been hard for your mother and you and Fraser. But you're right, Daisy and Clara needed to grieve too. But you were so young to have had that insight, especially when you were dealing with the shock of it all too. How on earth did you cope?'

He gave a loose-shouldered shrug. 'Someone had to cope. No one else was up to it.'

No wonder he locked his emotions away. No wonder he was strong and capable and self-reliant. He had to be. He had trained himself to stay in control at all times and in all circumstances. It made her admire him all the more to think he had put his own feelings to one side to consider the pain and suffering of others. He had searched for the higher ground in a difficult moral dilemma and he had stuck to his principles in spite of his own grief.

'Do you ever see them? Your half-sister and her mother?' she asked.

Mack put his wine glass down and gave a half-smile. 'I do, actually. Daisy's at university now, doing architecture. She's a bright girl. I'm really proud of all she has achieved.'

'She wasn't at Fraser's wedding?'

He shook his head, his smile disappearing, a frown taking its place. 'Sadly, no. Fraser has never shown any interest in being involved in Daisy's life.'

'But you've been a stalwart support to her and her mum all these years.' Elspeth posed it as a statement rather than a question because she was already certain of the answer. Mack would not have rejected them. He had too good a character to do something like that. It made her feelings for him blossom all the more. Feelings she had promised herself she would keep under control. But how could she stop feeling the way she did?

'Daisy and Clara are good people who had a bad thing happen to them. They had no idea my father had a double life. He'd kept us a secret from them just as he'd kept them a secret from us.' He gave a rough-edged sigh and added, 'I've lost count of the number of lies he must have told over the years. I thought I was close to him but sometimes I wonder if I knew him at all.'

'You can only know someone as well as they want you to know them,' Elspeth said.

'We all have parts of ourselves we would rather keep hidden.'

Mack gave another slanted smile and leaned forward to brush his fingers lightly over the back of her hand where it was resting on her knee. 'What parts of yourself do you like to keep hidden, hmm?' His grey-blue eyes meshed with hers with a steady intensity that made something slip sideways in her stomach.

One thing Elspeth was desperate to keep hidden was her developing feelings for him. Deep feelings that had no place in a fling such as theirs. Not according to the rules—*his* rules. But her heart had no time for his rules, it was on its own journey. Every moment she spent with him made it harder to ignore the way she felt about him. He had all the qualities she most admired in a man: steadiness, loyalty, commitment to those he cared about, moral fortitude—the list went on. She gave a tight smile and moved her hand away. 'My twin is the one with stuff she likes to keep hidden. I thought I was closer to her than anyone but I had no idea she had a one-night stand with your brother. She isn't a one-night-stand type of girl. But apparently she ran into her ex-fiancé that night with his latest lover and it upset her. I'm not sure why it should have upset her so much. She was the one who jilted him. It seems a little inconsistent to be feeling jealous when he takes up with a new lover. After all, it's been seven years. He's probably had dozens of lovers by now.'

'Do you think she still has feelings for him?'

Elspeth shrugged one shoulder and picked up her wine glass. 'She says not but sometimes people lie to themselves more than other people, right?'

'They do indeed.' Mack leaned back in his chair and took a sip of his wine, his gaze still trained on her.

The night sounds from the garden provided a peaceful background soundtrack. Crickets had joined the croaking frogs and the tinkling of the water feature added to the peaceful ambience. She couldn't remember a time when she had felt so close to someone other than her twin. The intimacy she and Mack had shared had enveloped her in a bubble of bliss and contentment she was loath to let go. How was she going to cope when their fling came to an end? She wished she could spend the rest of her life like this—relaxing in his easy company, her body tingling with the memory of his magical touch.

But Mack wasn't the happy-ever-after type. He was bruised by the betrayal of his father's double life. He was wary of long-term commitment, having seen the devastation of his mother when the truth about his father's mistress and love child had come out. It would have been a terrible shock to him, to see his beloved father in a completely different light. To lose his father in such tragic circumstances with so many issues left unresolved between them. But it didn't mean Mack had to shy away from finding true love himself. He would make such a wonderful life partner. He would be a kind and loving and supportive father to his children. Look at the way he supported and cared for his half-sister. It showed how deeply principled he was and Elspeth couldn't help admiring him for it.

'Mack?'

'Hmm?'

'You said you would have liked to pursue a different career other than take over your father's business interests. What was it you wanted to do?'

He put his wine glass down, his expression cast in shadowed lines. It seemed an age before he spoke, as if he was feeling compromised by talking about something he had let go a long time ago. 'I had dreams of becoming a professional musician.'

'What do you play?'

'The piano.'

'Do you still play? I didn't see a piano at Crannochbrae and there isn't one here.'

He gave a twisted smile. 'The one at Crannochbrae was sold after my father died. I haven't bothered replacing it since. I haven't played in years.'

'Do you miss it?'

'Not any more.'

'But you did?'

Something flickered through his gaze—a flash of a memory, a lingering emotion, a hint of regret. 'For a while but I had to be practical. It's hard to make money as a professional musician. And I had to make money, lots of money, or my family's estate would have been lost.'

Elspeth wondered what else he had given up in order to keep his family's assets on track. He had sacrificed his dream and his youth to protect his family as well as his father's mistress and love child. She stood from her chair and came over to place her hand on his broad shoulder, looking deep into his eyes. 'I think you're amazing, Mack.' Her voice was as whisper-soft as the light breeze that teased the nearby shrubbery.

His hand came up to encircle her wrist, his fingers warm and strong. He tugged her down to his lap, his arms going around her. His eyes moved back and forth between each of hers for endless moments, his breath catching as if he saw something in her gaze that affected him deeply. One of his hands began to stroke from between her shoulder blades to the base of her spine—long, slow, languorous strokes that triggered a sensual storm in her body. His mouth drifted closer as if in slow motion. Her breath caught in anticipation, her hands going to his broad shoulders, her heart kicking up its pace. His lips brushed hers in a barely there kiss. A feather-light touch that sent a tingle through her lips and straight to her core. He placed his mouth against hers again, firmer this time, his lips moving in a leisurely massaging motion that sent her pulse racing.

He lifted his mouth off hers, caught and held her gaze for a pulsing beat—an erotic silent interval that ramped up her need of him like a flame on dry tinder. He didn't say a word. He simply framed her face with his hands and kissed her again—a deep and passionate kiss that sent a shower of sparks down her spine. His tongue tangled with hers in a sexy dance that made her heart beat all the harder and faster.

Finally, he eased back to look at her, his own breathing heavy. 'I think you're pretty amazing too.' His voice had a rusty edge, his gaze warm and tender. So tender, she wondered if he was developing feelings for her. Or was she fooling herself? Mistaking raw passion for something else?

Elspeth traced a line around his sculptured mouth with her finger. 'Make love to me?'

He pressed a hot hard kiss to her mouth and stood, taking her with him. 'With pleasure,' he said, and carried her indoors.

# CHAPTER ELEVEN

MACK HEARD A faint buzzing during the night and rolled over in bed to see Elspeth reaching for her phone. She checked the screen and gave a deep sigh and turned the phone off, placing it on the bedside table.

'Who was it?'

She turned to him with a rueful expression. 'My mother.'

He frowned, and propped himself up on one elbow. 'Doesn't she realise what time it is?'

She began to chew at her lower lip, her gaze drifting away from his. 'I didn't tell her I was in France. She thinks I'm in Scotland, doing a tour on my own.' She flopped down on the pillows and released another sigh. 'She texts or calls dozens of times a day or night. I'm so tired of it, I usually turn off my phone but I forgot when we went to bed.'

Mack trailed his fingers down the silky

skin of her arm. 'She loves you and is probably worried about you.'

'I know but I can take care of myself. I'm not a little kid any more.'

'If you keep ignoring her calls and messages, she's going to worry even more. It's what mothers do—they worry.'

Elspeth turned her head on the pillow to look at him. 'What do you think I should do? Answer every one of them? I'd never get anything else done.'

Mack took her nearest hand and brought it up to his chest. 'Call her first. Let her know how you're doing. She's pursuing you because she's sensing you're pulling away. If you reach out to her instead it might rebalance things a bit. It's worth a try.'

'I guess…' She sounded doubtful.

Mack kissed each of her fingertips in turn, his gaze holding hers. 'Learning to let go is hard for some parents, especially when they've had good reason to worry in the past.'

'I know but I'm trying to live my own life now. She's spent the last twenty-six years fussing over me like I'm going to drop dead in front of her. I need to know who I am without her. I need autonomy but she won't let me go.'

Mack could only imagine the terror for a

parent having a child with a life-threatening allergy. His mother had told him of her fear the day he inhaled a peanut that went down to his lung. He had only been a toddler and had only the slightest memory of it but she had never forgotten it and every time she had spoken of it, he had sensed the raw unmitigated fear she had experienced that day. But Elspeth's mother had had many such harrowing days. Days when she would have been terrified that the anaphylaxis would take away her beloved child. 'I really don't know how parents cope with the stress of bringing up kids even without a life-threatening allergy. It seems like such a lot of hard work.'

Elspeth looked at him with her clear blue gaze. 'Don't you want to be a father one day?'

It wasn't the first time he'd been asked the question but it was the first time he paused for a moment over his answer. He had always ruled out having a family, figuring he'd been responsible for two already. But now, he allowed the thought some space in his mind…picturing what it would be like to hold a baby, his own baby, in his arms. A baby conceived out of love.

And there was that tricky word again— love. The word he avoided, the concept, the emotion he shied away from because it had already done enough damage in his life. Loving had led to hurt, to loss, to bitter disappointment. To scars that never quite healed.

'Mack?' Elspeth's soft voice broke through his moment of reflection.

He gave her hand a playful squeeze. 'Not right now.'

'But maybe one day?'

He shrugged. 'Who knows? What about you? Is becoming a mother important to you?'

A shadow passed over her features and she focussed her gaze on their joined hands. 'I'd be worried about a baby inheriting my allergy.'

'There's no guarantee it would, though.'

She gave a tight smile that was sad at the corners. 'And no guarantee it wouldn't. The genetic lottery being what it is.'

'There are worse things to have than a peanut allergy, surely?'

Elspeth turned on her side to face him. 'Twins?'

He stroked a finger down the cute slope of her nose. 'Was it hard being a twin?'

'No, not really. I adore my sister but while we might look exactly the same, we're completely different in personality.' She paused for a beat before adding, 'I found it hard to keep up with her, especially with Mum being so overprotective of me all the time. In some ways, Elodie got shoved aside. I guess that's why she always craved the spotlight because she certainly didn't get much attention from Mum. But then, Elodie got to do heaps of stuff I never could. Going to school, parties, playdates, that sort of thing. I lost confidence, became shy and introverted. My world shrank while hers expanded.'

Mack gently tucked a strand of her hair behind her ear. 'You have no reason to lack confidence. You're an accomplished young woman in your own right. And beautiful and sexy too.'

She gave a rueful grimace. 'I'm not sure I'm going to be so confident when I next have a lover.'

A sharp pain in his gut caught Mack off guard. But of course she would have another lover one day in the not too distant future. He might be her first but he wouldn't be her last. Not unless he changed the rules… The rules he had never thought of changing before.

He forced a smile and leaned down to press a light kiss to her lips. 'Go back to sleep. I have something special planned for the next few days.'

Her eyes lit up. 'What?'

'That's for me to know and for you to find out.'

Elspeth snuggled closer, her legs tangling with his. 'I'm not sure I'll be able to get back to sleep now you've got me all excited.'

*Right back at you, sweetheart.*

Mack wrapped his arms around her and for the next half an hour or so sleep was the last thing on his mind.

Over the next few days, Elspeth enjoyed discovering more about the village of Lagrasse. They went on walking tours of the village, picnics by the river and explored the Corbières wine region—the largest wine-producing region of France.

On the last day before they were due to go back home, Mack took her on a tour of the Abbey Sainte-Marie, informing her of its history and other interesting details about its construction.

'The construction of the abbey was given the go-ahead by Charlemagne in 783,' he said, walking hand in hand with her. 'The village developed later and is known for both the abbey and its bridges. The abbey was active from the eighth century until the French Revolution, when many monasteries were destroyed. After one hundred and fifty years of neglect, a restoration programme was established and what we see today is the result.'

'It's certainly magnificent,' Elspeth said, looking around her in wonder and awe.

Mack's arm went around her waist, drawing her close. 'I hope I'm not boring you with the history lesson?'

She smiled up at him. 'Me? Bored? You must be joking. I'm loving every minute.' She was loving every minute of being with him. He could be talking gibberish and she would still be loving it. But that was the trouble…she was loving not just the sound of his voice, not just the protection of his arm around her waist, not just the way he looked at her, not just the way he made love to her, but him.

She loved *him*.

The realisation was like a lightning flash, momentarily blinding her. How could she be so foolish as to fall in love with a man who had no interest in falling in love with anyone, much less her? And how could it be possible to fall in love with a man she had only met a handful of days ago? Was it even possible? Or had she let the romantic setting get to her?

Elspeth took a step forward but almost stumbled and Mack's arm quickly tightened around her waist. 'Are you okay?' he asked with a look of concern.

She forced a smile and touched a hand to her warm face. 'I'm fine. But perhaps a little thirsty.'

'Come on.' He led her to the nearest exit. 'Let's get a drink and something to eat.'

A short time later they were seated in one of the cafés in the central square of the village. The square was surrounded by beautiful houses, their facades dating back centuries and adding to the old-world charm of the village. Elspeth sipped at a glass of mineral water and Mack had coffee while they waited for their food to arrive. She was conscious of his gaze resting on her, his expression still etched in lines of concern.

'Feeling any better?'

Elspeth put her glass down and smiled. 'I'm perfectly fine. I've enjoyed everything you've shown me. I wish we had another day or two to see more.'

There was a small silence.

'We could extend our stay,' Mack said, picking up his coffee cup and cradling it in his cupped palm. 'I can take a bit more time off work. A day or two at least. How about you?'

Elspeth ran the tip of her tongue over her

lips. 'Are you sure you can spare the time? I guess I could ask for another day or two off work. But aren't you worried about your brother? Have you heard how he's doing?'

He put his cup down again. 'He called me this morning when you were in the shower. Sabine's father has decided to keep him on after all.'

Elspeth frowned. 'Really? But how does Sabine feel about that? Won't she feel her father is being disloyal to her?'

Mack shrugged one broad shoulder. 'Sabine's father is like a lot of hard-nosed businessmen—they don't let emotions get in the way of a good business decision. He's been impressed with Fraser's work. That would be his deciding factor in keeping him on, not whether or not it upsets Sabine.'

Elspeth reached for the last of her mineral water. 'I wonder if he's hoping they'll get back together again. But unfaithfulness is a tough thing to forgive.'

'Yes. And trust hard to build up again.'

Their food arrived at that point and the conversation switched to other things. But Elspeth had only taken a couple of bites of her salad when she felt a tingling in her mouth, then, within a second or two, her tongue began to swell along with her throat.

Panic gripped at her chest, her breathing becoming laboured, her heart rate escalating, a sweat breaking out on her body. She dropped her fork with a clatter and looked around for her bag. 'Quick. I need my EpiPen.'

Mack was out of his chair so fast it fell over backwards with a noisy clatter. He rushed around to get her bag off the floor, quickly searching for the EpiPen and then handing it to her. 'Can you do it or do you want me to do it for you?' His voice was calm but she could see the worry in his gaze.

'I can do it...' She grabbed the EpiPen and jabbed herself in the thigh and within seconds her heart began to race and a wave of intense anxiety washed over her as the epinephrine raised her blood pressure and opened her airways. And then, she stopped thinking as the effect of the drug clouded her mind and rendered her body useless...

With one hand on her shoulder, Mack whipped out his phone and called for an ambulance. He could barely get his voice to work to give clear instructions to the emergency service personnel. His heart was hammering, a cold sweat breaking out over his body. He couldn't lose her. He couldn't let her die. She had to live. She had to survive. The panic built in

his chest until he could scarcely inflate his
lungs. He bent down and lowered her into the
recovery position, gently soothing her, trying to keep the raging panic out of his voice.
'They're on their way. Stay with me, that's a
good girl. You're doing fine.'

*Please let her be doing fine*, he prayed, to
a God he hadn't prayed to since he was a kid.

Within a short time an ambulance came
wailing into the village square and Elspeth
was loaded in, with Mack accompanying her.
The plan was to take her to the emergency
department of the hospital in the nearby town
of Carcassonne. The paramedics monitored
her, giving her oxygen and another shot of
epinephrine when her vital signs deterio-
rated.

The wailing of the ambulance siren rang
inside Mack's head, ramping up his panic
to an unbearable level. What if she didn't
make it? What if there wasn't a doctor there
who knew what to do? She looked so pale
and sweaty, almost lifeless. His gut tied itself into hard knots—knots that twisted and
turned until his stomach burned with pain.
A pain that crept higher, higher, higher until
it wrapped an iron band around his heart.
How could he lose her? It couldn't be pos-

sible. It must *not* be possible. He had never felt so powerfulness, so out of control, so bereft at the thought of her not making it. It reminded him of the day his father died, that terrible day he could never quite erase from his memory. The piercing screams of his mother, the ambulance siren wailing up the driveway—a pointless arrival for there was nothing anyone could do by that stage. Mack had watched them wheel his father out on a stretcher. He hadn't even been able to say goodbye. The words had been locked in his throat, so he'd swallowed them, shoving them deep inside him, along with his feelings. He had learned that day his feelings were of no use in a crisis. He had to be strong and in control to get everyone else through the worst time of their lives.

This was another one of those times.

They finally got to the hospital and Mack had to step out of the way as they took her inside. He gave what information he could to the admission staff, relieved he spoke fluent French. Doubly relieved when the doctor came out and said Elspeth was going to be fine but they were going to admit her overnight for observation.

'I want to stay with her,' he insisted. The

words echoed in his head for the next few minutes until he was allowed entry to her room.

*I want to stay with her. I want to stay with her. I want to stay with her.*

Elspeth came out of her drug-induced stupor to see Mack sitting by her bedside. His features were haggard and his hair looked as if his hands had been through it many times, for it was sticking up every which way. 'The doctor said you insisted on staying overnight with me but you don't have to.'

'I'm not leaving you and that's final.' His tone was so strident, even if she'd had the energy to argue with him, she wouldn't have bothered. But in her weakened state, she was secretly glad he was going to be with her. Having anaphylaxis at any time was terrifying but having it while in a foreign country even more so. She was just grateful Mack had acted so swiftly and not gone into a panic himself as her father used to do.

She lay back on the pillows and closed her eyes, exhausted from the drama and fear, her body still recovering from the dose of epinephrine. But also painfully embarrassed at how things had turned out. She should have double-checked the menu but her French wasn't anywhere near as fluent as Mack's. There must have been nut contamination in her salad or in the dressing.

'Mack?'

His hand gave hers a gentle squeeze. 'I'm here, *m'eudail*. Try to rest now.'

'I'm sorry…'

'It's not your fault. If it's anyone's it's mine. I should've ordered for you. I didn't think.' His tone was ragged around the edges and full of self-recrimination.

Elspeth tried to open her eyes to look at him but overwhelming tiredness got the better of her. She gave a wobbly sigh and drifted off…

# CHAPTER TWELVE

MACK BROUGHT HER limp hand up to his mouth, pressing his lips to her fingers. His chest was tight as a drum, his lungs too cramped to draw in a decent breath. He blamed himself for not being vigilant enough. Elspeth had a life-threatening allergy and seeing her like that, struggling to breathe, was confronting. Not just confronting but terrifying. What if it had happened when they were out of reach of a hospital? What if she hadn't brought her EpiPens with her? Over the last few days, he'd almost forgotten about her allergy. He'd been so caught up with spending time with her, making love to her, knowing their fling was coming to an end, as all his flings did.

But seeing her so ill had shaken him to the core. Making him realise he didn't want their fling to end like all the others.

*I want to stay with her.*

He had grown close to her in a way he

hadn't expected, closer than anyone else he had ever met. Not just physically close but forming a deep connection that opened his heart to possibilities he had never considered before—possibilities he had never wanted to consider. He had never asked anyone to live with him before. That had always been a step too far. It reeked too much of commitment and he didn't do commitment.

Almost losing her had shocked him into realising he had developed feelings for her. The sort of feelings that he had never felt for anyone else. He wasn't ready to call it love, the sort of love that romantics went on about. But he cared deeply for her. Why else had he panicked as he'd never panicked before seeing her struggling for air? He couldn't imagine not seeing her again. He had already extended their fling another day or two. What would it hurt to extend it a little longer? A little longer than he had ever done before? It would be a practical solution, a convenient arrangement that would give them a little more time to enjoy each other's company. How much longer was not something he could answer with any definitiveness, which was unusual for him. But he didn't put too much significance on that. He was not going to let things get out of control.

Mack shuffled his chair closer to Elspeth's bedside and gently stroked her hair back from her forehead. Her face was pale, her features relaxed in sleep, and his heart squeezed as if it were in a cruel vice. His throat thickened, unfamiliar emotions rising in his chest. 'I'm not going anywhere,' he said in a rough whisper. 'You're stuck with me for a while longer.'

Elspeth woke a couple of times during the night when the nurse on duty came in to do a set of obs. And every time, she saw Mack sitting beside her bed, wide awake with his concerned gaze on her. Once the nurse left, Elspeth turned to him. 'Have you had any sleep at all?'

'No.'

She ran her gaze over his weary features. His eyes were darkly shadowed, his jaw was heavily peppered with regrowth, his skin looked paler than normal and there were fine lines around his mouth she had never noticed before. 'You look terrible.'

'Thank you.' His tone was dry.

She plucked at the starched white sheet covering her. 'I bet I don't look too crash hot either.'

He grasped her hand and kissed her bent

knuckles, his eyes meshing with hers. 'You look as beautiful as ever.'

Her heart swelled at the tenderness in his gaze. 'Thanks for staying with me. It's usually my mum who sits there hour after hour.'

He suddenly frowned. 'I should have thought to call her. And your sister. Do you want me to do it now or—?'

'No, I'm quite safe with you and I don't want to stress them.'

'Will you tell them once we get back home?'

'Maybe.'

'I can see why your mother panics,' Mack said, stroking her hand. 'You scared the hell out of me.' He swallowed deeply and added in a husky tone, 'I'm not going to be game enough to let you out of my sight after this.'

Elspeth gave a lopsided smile. 'You're going to have to though, soon, aren't you?' She looked back down at the sheet she was toying with. 'We're having a fling, not a long-term relationship. Those were the rules. Your rules.'

There was a pulsing silence.

'What if I wanted to tweak the rules?'

She looked at him in shock. 'What do you mean?'

He grasped her hand even more firmly as

if worried she would pull away. 'I don't want our fling to end just yet. I want to continue seeing you.'

Elspeth ran her tongue over her suddenly dry lips. He wanted to extend their fling? 'What time frame were you thinking?' For there would be a time frame, of that she was sure. He would not be offering her a for-ever relationship, a full-time commitment such as marriage. It was probably silly of her to expect it given they had only known each other such a short time. But a part of her longed for such a commitment from him anyway. For she knew how she felt, she was sure of her love for him. The trouble was knowing for sure if love was behind his offer, or simple lust. The health scare he had witnessed had created a sense of urgency and drama, which had probably coloured if not downright influenced his decision to extend their fling. Dramatic circumstances experienced by a couple often had that effect—made them draw closer together for a time—but it didn't always last, not unless deep and lasting love underpinned it.

And how could she be sure it did?

'We can take it a day at a time,' Mack said. 'Just enjoy each other's company as we've been doing.'

Elspeth was trying to figure out how such an arrangement would work in reality. He was based in Scotland, she in England. She had a job she adored, a flat she had not long rented. A year-long lease she had only just signed. How would her mother cope if she moved out of London? Judging by the number of missed calls and text messages she'd received from her, Elspeth doubted her mother would ever agree to her moving to Scotland. And could she even be sure she would get a position in another library, especially at such short notice? What exactly did Mack expect of her? 'I don't know, Mack…' She softened it with a smile. 'We live in different parts of the UK. I don't want to quit my job or—'

'I'm not asking you to quit, just ask for a transfer,' he said. 'We'll figure the details out later but, for now, I want you to get well and at least consider moving in with me for a few weeks when we get back home.'

Her eyebrows shot up. 'Move in with you?'

'Why are you so surprised? It makes sense to cohabit for the sake of convenience. It's way more practical than trying to conduct a long-distance relationship.'

But whose convenience was he talking about? It certainly wouldn't be convenient for her, not unless he was willing to commit his whole heart to her. 'I'm not sure I'm ready for such a big step...' she began. Not unless she was sure his feelings for her were the same as hers for him. 'You're probably only asking because of what happened. It scared you and you think you need to take care of me, but you don't. I can take care of myself.'

'Why don't you think about it for the rest of the day?' he suggested. 'We don't fly home until tomorrow. You can decide then.' He rose from the chair and pressed a kiss to her forehead, sweeping her hair back in a tender gesture as he straightened. 'I'm going to let you sleep while I head back and have a shower and a shave. You should be ready for discharge by the time I get back.'

'Okay.' She sank back against the pillows with a sigh. 'I'll think about it.'

Mack walked out of the hospital with a spring in his step. The convenience of having her move in with him was his primary motivation for asking her. And he was confident Elspeth would agree once she'd had time to consider it. She was young and inexperienced, so it was a big step for her, but he didn't want their fling to end any time soon and he was sure neither did she.

He stopped off to buy her a gift on the way back to the villa to lift her spirits. Her health scare had obviously deeply unsettled her, as it had him. His gut still churned as he recalled the harrowing moment at the café when she went into anaphylaxis. Her life could have ended then and there and *that* didn't bear thinking about. He couldn't imagine losing her. She had only been in his life such a short time—a matter of days—and yet he had developed feelings for her that he had not experienced for anyone else before. They were so unfamiliar to him he didn't know how to describe them.

All he knew was, he wanted her with him for much longer than a casual fling.

The jeweller's assistant showed Mack a diamond and sapphire ensemble of pendant, earrings and an engagement ring. He hadn't asked to be shown an engagement ring and wondered why the woman had brought one out. *Sheesh.* The French were such romantics. He glanced at the ring with its winking solitaire diamond and deep blue sapphires and then back at the middle-aged woman serving him. 'I won't need the ring, just the pendant and earrings.'

The older woman raised her brows over

twinkly raisin-dark eyes. 'No? Maybe *monsieur* will come back for it another time?'

Mack gave a stiff smile. *'C'est impossible.'*

Elspeth came back to the villa with Mack later that day. He was attentive and solicitous with only marginally less fussing over her than her mother would do. He helped get her comfortable on a lounger on a shady section of the terrace and then brought her out a refreshing cup of tea and a plate of fresh fruit.

'Here you go.' He set it down next to her. 'Is there anything else I can get you?'

'No. This is lovely, thanks.'

He reached for something inside his white chinos' pocket. 'I bought you a little gift.' He handed her a rectangular dark blue velvet jewellery case. 'I hope you like them.'

Elspeth took the box with bated breath. The box was too large to be a ring box and she was annoyed with herself for even hoping a ring could be in there. She prised open the lid to find a beautiful diamond and sapphire pendant and matching droplet earrings. They were stunningly beautiful, quite easily the most gorgeous she had ever seen. She didn't dare think about how much they had cost. Her twin was used to wearing ridiculously expensive jewellery, but Elspeth was not and wondered if she ever could. 'Oh, my goodness… Oh, Mack, you shouldn't have. I can't accept these. They're too much.'

'Don't be ridiculous. I want you to have them. Consider them a "get well" gift.'

Elspeth glanced up at him as a thought occurred to her. An uncomfortable thought that triggered a tiny flicker of anger. 'Are you sure they're not a bribe?'

He gave a sudden frown. 'A bribe? What do you mean?'

She closed the lid of the box with a little snap and handed it back to him. 'I know what you're doing. You want me to move in with you and this is a way to convince me. But I don't want gifts.'

'What do you want?' His voice had a raw edge to it, but his expression was shuttered. And he ignored the box in her outstretched hand.

Elspeth put the box on the table next to the lounger, and then swung her legs over so she was in a sitting position. 'I want more than expensive jewellery. I want to know how you feel about me.'

'I told you how I feel about you. I enjoy your company. I like being with you. I care about you.'

Elspeth rose from the lounger to put some

distance between them. 'You barely know me, Mack. We only met a handful of days ago. And for part of that I was pretending to be my twin. How can you be sure you care about me, the real me?'

Mack stood and came over to her, taking both of her hands in his. 'I know the real you. That's who I've developed feelings for—you, only you.'

'Are you saying you're in love with me?'

There was a beat or two of silence. Too long a silence. A heartbreaking silence that told her all she needed to know.

'I'm saying I'd like our fling to continue for as long as we both enjoy each other's company.' His expression remained inscrutable but she sensed a carefully restrained tension in him.

'I know how silly this is going to sound but I can't accept your offer,' Elspeth said, pulling her hands out of his. 'I want more than a let's-see-how-it-goes relationship. I want more than someone to enjoy my company. I want more than someone to care about me. I want the sort of love that most people aspire to. But you've ruled that sort of love out. The love that binds two people together for a lifetime.'

He sent one of his hands through his hair

in an agitated manner. 'Isn't it a little too early to be talking about marriage?'

She gave him a challenging look. 'Would there ever be a time when you'd be agreeable to talk about it? You said you never wanted to settle down. You've already ruled out the possibility, so how can I wait in hope that you might one day change your mind?'

He walked over to the edge of the terrace, standing with his back towards her, his gaze focussed on the view of the abbey in the distance. 'Marriage is not something I'm willing to discuss, now or in the future.' He turned to face her, his face set in intractable lines. 'I'm offering you a relationship for the time being. That's all.'

'I'm flattered by your offer but you'll have to forgive me for declining it,' Elspeth said. 'If our feelings aren't the same for each other, what would be the point? We'd be wasting each other's time and, quite frankly, I feel I've wasted enough years of my life already. I need to take charge of my own destiny and not wait around hoping good things will come my way. I have to go out and find those good things. And one of those good things I most desire is to be loved for me. As I am, allergy and all.'

His dark eyebrows shot together. 'You

surely don't think I'm holding back on marriage because of your allergy? For God's sake, Elspeth, didn't you see how worried I was about you? You almost gave me a heart attack collapsing like that. The thought of losing you is what triggered me into asking you to come and live with me. I want to take care of you.'

She slowly shook her head at him. 'If I allowed you to do that, I would be simply exchanging you for my mother. I'm not your responsibility, Mack. I want to be much more than a liability you feel pressured to take on out of guilt. I want to be your equal, your partner in life, not a temporary interest that has no possibility of a long-term future.'

He muttered a curse word not quite under his breath. 'So where do we go from here? You want out? Now?'

Elspeth gave a deep sigh. 'I think it's for the best, don't you? Why prolong something that's going to end anyway? You were only attracted to me because I was playing the role of my twin. That's what first got your attention but that's not who I am. I don't wear designer clothes and exotic perfume and sky-high heels. I'm not a party girl who can work a room. I'm a shy and introverted homebody who doesn't belong in your world. If we continued our fling, you'd soon get tired of me, I'm sure. I'd rather we part now as friends.'

'Friends?' His top lip curled, his eyes flashed, his jaw tightened. 'I don't need you as a friend.'

'The thing is, Mack, you don't need anyone, not in an emotional sense. You won't allow yourself to.'

'What do you feel for me?' The question blindsided her for a moment, especially when it was delivered in such a blunt tone with zero expression on his face. He was like a robot, an emotionless robot programmed to issue commands but with no capacity to feel.

Elspeth knotted her hands in front of her body, wary of revealing too much of her feelings for him when there was no possibility of them ever being returned. 'I've enjoyed being with you. You've taught me so much, not just about sex but life in general. I enjoyed this time here in Lagrasse, in spite of my health scare. I will always look back on our time together with…with fondness.'

His top lip went up again. 'Fondness?' His tone was cynical. 'Is that all? And yet, here you are practically begging me to get down on bended knee and offer you a marriage proposal.'

A streak of anger rippled down her spine.

'What you offered me was a proposition, one that's probably not unlike the one your father offered to his mistress. I suspect he kept her going for years with false promises, fanning her hopes with each little gift when he visited, making her think that one day, her dream would finally be fulfilled, that they would live happily ever after. But it didn't happen, did it? He was unable to love either her or your mother the way they wanted to be loved.'

'Please do not bring my father into this discussion.' His words came out through thinned lips, his tone embittered, his gaze diamond hard.

'We both have father wounds, Mack,' Elspeth said, softly, realising it with a flash of insight. 'We were both let down by our fathers, betrayed, rejected and abandoned by them. But that doesn't mean we have to live our lives frightened of others betraying, rejecting or abandoning us. We have to be courageous enough to ask for what we want, to not be afraid to embrace it when it happens to come our way. To not short-change ourselves in the fear of losing the one thing we crave above all else—love.'

Mack strode back to the balustrade of the terrace, his hands gripping the stone with white-knuckled force. His back was rigid with tension, his shoulders hunched forward as he fought for control. 'All right.' He turned back to face her, his face still devoid of emotion. 'I'll change our flights for this evening. There's no point staying another night when you're so keen to leave.'

'You don't have to do that, Mack. One more night won't—'

'On the contrary, I do have to do it. I'll book your flight for London. I'll fly to Edinburgh. We won't have to see each other again after today.'

He turned and walked down the steps leading into the garden, disappearing from sight before she could think of a single thing to say. But what could she say that hadn't already been said? Wasn't it easier, less painful this way? A clean cut was better than a long drawn-out goodbye.

There was next to no conversation between them on the way to the airport later that day, but there was a surfeit of tension. Elspeth could feel it pulsing between them in the air in invisible waves.

As they were waiting for their flights to be called to the gate, Elspeth looked up at him. 'Mack? Please don't let us end this way.'

His expression was set in tight lines, his mouth a thin line. 'It was your choice to end it. Not mine.'

'You're being unfair. I don't want to end it with any bad feelings between us. The least we could do is part on good terms.'

'All right, then.' He offered her his hand in a formal handshake. 'Goodbye. I hope you have a pleasant flight.' It was the sort of thing he might say to a stranger he had just met, or a business associate he had nothing in common with other than work. Not the sort of farewell one would say to one's lover, a lover who had shared his bed, his body. He was her first lover. Her first love. Her only love.

Elspeth slipped her hand into his and tried to ignore the tingle his touch evoked in her flesh and the arrow of pain in her heart that this was the last time she would feel his touch. A wave of grief swept over her, making tears sting at the backs of her eyes and a lump rise in her throat. 'Goodbye, Mack. Thank you for everything you've done for me. I really enjoyed getting to know you.'

He was still holding her hand, his gaze shuttered. 'You've got your new EpiPens with you?'

She patted her tote bag with her free hand. 'Yes.'

His gaze drifted to her mouth, his throat rising and falling over a tight swallow. 'Right, well then, I'd better let you go. Your flight is due to board any second now.'

Elspeth pulled her hand out of his and forced a smile. 'Right. Don't want to miss it.'

He seemed to hesitate for a long moment, just staring at her without speaking. But then, he took her by the upper arms and pulled her close and planted a brief but firm kiss to her lips. 'Stay safe, *m'eudail*.' His voice had lost its brisk impersonality and instead was deep and husky.

'I will.' Elspeth turned to join her departure-lounge queue but when she glanced over her shoulder, Mack was gone.

Mack strode down the concourse of the airport to his own departure gate willing himself not to look back. He never looked back when he left a fling. And that was all his relationship with Elspeth was, wasn't it? A fling. A fling that hadn't gone the way he'd wanted and that stuck in his craw in a way he didn't like. He was usually the one who decided when a relationship was going to end. He liked the sense of control it gave him to have the power to pull the plug when it suited him. He didn't like surprises and

Elspeth rejecting his offer to move in with him was an unpleasant surprise. A shock, a gut-wrenching disappointment that he couldn't explain other than it had thwarted his plans. He had envisaged a few weeks, possibly months of being together, enjoying the passion that had fired between them. He wasn't the settling-down type, marriage was not and never had been in his plans. He had no wish to commit to one person for the rest of his life. His mother had done that and it had all but destroyed her to find the object of her love had betrayed her in the most despicable way. Love had destroyed his mother as it had Clara and to a lesser degree Daisy, his half-sister. It had certainly contributed to the wayward behaviour of his brother, which had continued to this day. Loving someone gave them the power to hurt you, to wound you, to destroy you.

And he was not going to allow anyone to do that to him.

Ever.

# CHAPTER THIRTEEN

ELSPETH HAD ONLY been home a matter of hours when Elodie turned up. She breezed in with her usual whirlwind restless energy and plonked herself down on the squishy sofa, curling her slim legs beneath her. 'It was all for nothing,' she said without preamble. 'The financial backers pulled out. I'm back where I started unless I can find someone else to fund my label. And that's hardly likely now everyone knows I'm the one who caused Fraser MacDiarmid's wedding to be cancelled.'

'I'm so sorry,' Elspeth said, curling up next to her. 'But things kind of backfired for me too.'

Elodie made a *poor you* moue with her mouth. 'So, your little fling with the Laird of Crannochbrae came to an end?'

Elspeth picked up one of the scatter cushions and began to toy with the ribbed hem. 'I ended it, actually.'

'Why?'

'Because for the first part of our time together, he thought I was you. I wasn't convinced he liked me for me.'

'You mean he found out you were you and not me? What, did you tell him? You promised me you wouldn't.'

'He guessed before I told him.'

'Did anyone else guess?'

'No, only him.'

'Smart guy.'

'Yes, very. I think he suspected something right from the start even though I was doing my level best to be you.'

Elodie gave a tinkly bell laugh. 'I would have loved to be a fly on the wall, especially when Fraser saw you.'

Elspeth gave a mock glower. 'I'm not sure I've quite forgiven you for not telling me about him.'

'Sorry about that but I just wanted to forget it ever happened.'

'Having met him, I can understand that. But Mack is nothing like him. He's so rock steady and hard-working and he's sacrificed so much for his family.'

'So why did you end it with him if you liked him so much?'

'Because I wanted more.'

'More as in what?'

'More as in love.'

Elodie leaned forward, her expression incredulous. 'Are you saying you're in love with him?'

Elspeth tossed the cushion to one side. 'I know it probably sounds ridiculous, but I think I fell in love with him more or less straight away.'

Elodie bounced off the sofa as if there were an ejector button beneath her. 'For pity's sake, Els, you can't possibly fall in love that quickly. You're a little star-struck by him, that's all. You have so little experience with men, no wonder you fancy yourself in love with him. I was like that with Lincoln. He was so charming and suave it blew me away but look how that ended.'

'I might not have as much experience as you do, but I know what I feel. He wanted me to move in with him. That would have meant me quitting my job and uprooting my life to live with him in Scotland. How would Mum cope with that?'

'You have to stop worrying about Mum. It's your life and you have to live it the way you want.'

'I know and what I want is someone to love me. To be brave enough to at least be open to the possibility. Mack doesn't want to settle down, and he's ruled out the possibility of ever falling in love.'

'It doesn't mean he won't fall in love,' Elodie said. 'The more those hardened playboys protest, the harder they fall.' She plonked back down on the sofa. 'I'm glad you're back, though. I was dreading someone taking a picture of you with Mack and people thinking it was me.'

Elspeth frowned. 'Why were you so worried about that?'

Elodie shrugged. 'My reputation is already shot to pieces. I don't need any more scandals attached to my name.' She blew out a long breath and added, 'But thanks for stepping in for me at the wedding. I'm sure you did a great job of being me.'

'Too good a job, it seems.' Elspeth sighed.

Mack filled his days with work, trying to distract himself from the emptiness he was feeling. He didn't want to admit how much he missed Elspeth. He hadn't realised how much he enjoyed her company until she was no longer in his life.

*No longer in his life...*

How those words tortured him in his darkest moments. It had been her choice to leave.

He had offered her a relationship and she had chosen not to take it. That was her privilege—he didn't want anyone to stay with him out of a sense of duty.

But why *did* he want her to stay with him? The sex was great, better than great. Amazing, the best he had ever had. The physical connection with her had shown him something about himself he hadn't realised before. He'd had sex with his previous partners but he had *made love* with Elspeth. Her inexperience had been part of it, but he suspected there was more to it than that. She gave of herself so trustingly and he had worshipped her body, treating it with such reverence, which had made their lovemaking rise to a different level—a level of awareness, of sensual feeling that transcended the physical. He missed the physical connection, but he missed even more the companionship, the conversation and emotional connection he had with her.

*Emotional?*

Mack mulled over the word, allowing it a little more space in his brain than he normally would. He was so used to dismissing emotions, masking them, denying them, eradicating them, that it was strange to give his mind permission to examine how he actually felt. He had blunted his feelings for years. Bludgeoned and smothered them in order to survive the aftermath of his father's death. He hadn't had time to grieve, he'd had to spring into action and help everyone else with their process of grieving. His mother, his brother, his father's mistress and his half-sister.

But what about him?

Elspeth had mentioned something about them both having a father wound. Mack had dismissed it at the time as psychobabble, yet another trendy term that had no relevance to him. But he realised now that his father's death had left its mark—a deep scar on his heart that had practically shut it down for fear of more hurt. He had forgotten how to access his emotions. He could barely recognise the feelings other people took for granted. There were so many feelings he had buried and he had been too scared to dig down to find them.

Being back at Crannochbrae reminded him of himself. A fortress, secure against the elements, strong and capable of withstanding the harshest weather and yet the rooms inside were just rooms, tastefully decorated and functional but without heart. He was like the suit of armour in the foyer—cold, hard and empty.

Mack wandered into what used to be the music room, which, for years now, was a sitting room filled with sofas and whatnot tables and priceless artwork and so on but lacking the one thing that had once set it apart. It had been a long time since his fingers had touched a piano keyboard.

Too long.

Maybe it was time to do something about that.

Elspeth was on a lunch break from work in a local café when she looked up to see Sabine standing next to her table. She put her coffee cup down with a tiny clatter. 'Sabine? How are you?'

Sabine gripped the top of the chair opposite Elspeth's. 'I wanted to see you.'

But who exactly did Sabine want to see? Her or Elodie? Had anyone told her of the switch? Had Mack?

'Please, sit down. Can I get you a coffee or something?'

'Maybe later.' Sabine pulled out the chair and sat, her gaze fixed on Elspeth's. 'I can see the difference now but back at Crannochbrae it was impossible.'

'Did Mack tell you who I really was?'

'No, Elodie called me yesterday and apologised for everything.'

'Oh, I'm so glad. I know she never intended for you to get hurt. And nor did I. I was aghast when I found out about—'

Sabine held up her hand like a stop sign. 'Please don't mention Fraser's name. I'm still furious with my father for keeping him on in the business.'

'That must be awful for you.'

She sighed and put her phone on the table, two of her fingers doing a slow little tap dance on the glittery cover. 'I'm kind of used to it, to be honest.' She stopped tapping her fingers and met Elspeth's gaze. 'Dad isn't the sensitive type. I thought Fraser was nothing like him, but I was wrong. Dad's had numerous affairs and my mother always turns a blind eye. I'm ashamed of how blind I was to Fraser's faults, but I liked how he needed me. I made him feel good and that made me feel good. But true love is a two-way thing, right? One person can't be doing all the emotional work. It has to be balanced.'

'I couldn't agree more,' Elspeth said. 'I'm so sorry for deceiving you. As soon as I met you I liked you. And when I met Fraser, I was worried you were going to be unhappy in the long run.'

Sabine gave a twisted smile. 'I'll be all right. Plenty more fish in the sea and all that. But how about you? It can't have been pleasant being slut-shamed by the press when you were completely innocent.'

'Yes, well, Mack made sure I was out of the firing line for a few days.'

There was a little silence.

Sabine's eyes began to twinkle. 'So, how was that?'

Elspeth could feel her cheeks heating enough to froth the milk for a cappuccino. 'It was…actually, I'd rather not talk about it. I'm sorry.' Tears stung at the backs of her eyes and a thickness in her throat made it hard to breathe. She could barely think of those few days with Mack without breaking down. She missed him so much. Her body ached for him. Her life seemed so empty and lonely without him in it. Was he missing her? Or had he moved on already by now? Going back to his playboy lifestyle as easily as taking his next breath.

Sabine reached for her hand across the table and gave it a supportive squeeze. 'I thought you two had a special connection. Are you going to see him again?'

Elspeth shook her head. 'I don't think it's wise. We want different things out of life.'

Sabine leaned back in her chair, her expression thoughtful. 'I don't know... Mack seemed really drawn to you.'

Elspeth gave her a wry look. 'That's because I was pretending to be Elodie.'

Sabine frowned. 'But he knew you had switched places. He was the only one who guessed. Elodie told me when she called me yesterday.'

'Yes, but he's only interested in a short-term fling. I want the fairy tale.'

Sabine sighed and picked up the cardboard menu that was propped up against the salt and pepper shakers on the table. 'Don't we all?'

Mack spent the next three weeks travelling as he saw to various business interests. The evenings he spent alone in his hotel room. He wasn't in the mood for socialising, he had no interest in pursuing a hook-up. His gut churned at the thought of sleeping with anyone other than Elspeth. How had he been satisfied with such impersonal hook-ups all these years? It made him feel ashamed of himself, that he had settled for such shallow encounters when he could have enjoyed a deeper connection.

A connection he still missed.

He got back home to Crannochbrae to find the piano he had ordered had been delivered and tuned. He sat down at the shiny black instrument and stretched his fingers out in front of him. Years had passed since he had played. Too many years. Could he even do it now? He had memorised whole sonatas in the past, pages and pages of music filed away in his brain. Could he access those notes now or had the years wiped them away?

He took a deep breath and placed his fingers on the keys. He began playing Debussy's 'Clair de Lune', the hauntingly beautiful cadences filling the music room, unlocking something in his chest. He continued to play, losing himself in the moment…or was he finding himself? The music spoke to him on a cellular level. It was part of who he used to be and yet he had not allowed it any room in his life for years. He hadn't realised how much he had missed it until now, when he was playing again.

And that was not the only thing he missed.

His body throbbed with a persistent ache for the feel of Elspeth's arms around him. He longed to see her clear blue eyes looking into his. He longed to feel her soft mouth crushed beneath his, her body welcoming him with such enthusiasm and sweet trust it made his heart contract even more than the music he was playing.

*His heart...*

His fingers paused on the keys, the press of his last notes giving an eerie echo in the music room. Since when had his heart been involved in his casual relationships? Never, not until Elspeth. She had opened him to the possibility of feeling something for someone other than lust. He realised with a jolt that the emptiness he was feeling was because he loved her. He was unfamiliar with the emotion in this context. Of course, he had loved his parents and still loved his brother, and Clara and Daisy also had a special place in his affections and always would.

But no one had captured his heart like sweet, shy Elspeth. She had unlocked his frozen heart, making him need her far more than physically. He needed her emotionally. He needed to be with her, to share his life with her, all the ups and downs and trials and triumphs that, up until this point, he had been experiencing alone. Without her, he was an empty music room without a piano. A suit of armour without a body.

But he was no longer willing to be a cold, hard, empty suit of armour. He was a living breathing man with a beating heart—a heart that beat for a young woman who was perfect for him in every way. He couldn't let another day pass without seeing her. Without telling her how he felt, how he had felt from almost the moment he'd met her. He had sensed she was his other half. The one person who could encourage him to be the person he was meant to be.

Elspeth was walking home from work with her head bowed down against the driving wind and rain. She had forgotten to bring an umbrella and the cold needles of rain were pricking her face like tiny darts of ice.

A tall figure appeared in front of her and she looked up to see Mack carrying a large umbrella. Shock swept through her. She had never expected to see him again. She blinked a couple of times to make sure she hadn't conjured him up out of desperation. But no, it really was him. Her heart leapt, her pulse raced, her hopes sprouted baby wings. 'Mack?' She couldn't keep the surprise out of her voice, couldn't stop the hammering of her heart, the ballooning of her hopes.

He placed the umbrella over her head.

'May I escort you home?' His deep mellifluous voice with its gorgeous Scottish accent almost made her swoon on the spot. How she had missed him! But why was he here in London? She knew he occasionally came down for business, but her place of work was a long way from the business district he worked in. Had he made a special trip to see her? But why?

'Oh, thanks. I didn't realise it was going to rain.' Elspeth fell into step beside him, her heart beating harder than the rain pattering down on the skin of the umbrella above them. 'What brings you to London? Business?'

He stopped walking and held her in place under the shelter of the umbrella with a gentle hand on her arm. 'I came to see you.'

Elspeth looked up into his grey-blue eyes and those baby wings of hope in her chest began to flutter. 'Why?'

Mack gave a crooked smile. 'Because I can't live another day without seeing your beautiful face. I've missed you, *m'eudail*. Ever since we parted in France, I've been moping around like a wounded bear. I can't believe it's taken me this long to realise I love you.'

Elspeth gaped at him in shock. 'Did you

say *love*?' She was dreaming…surely she was dreaming. The rain must have soaked through to her brain and turned it to mush.

He brought her closer, somehow juggling the umbrella above their heads while the rain cascaded down around them, hitting the footpath in loud plops and splatters. 'I love you with every fibre of my being. You are the one person, the only person who has opened my heart to love. You were right, I was too afraid to harbour the possibility of loving someone. I was too afraid of being vulnerable, of one day losing that love. But loving someone always comes with a risk. But I'm prepared to take that risk now, but only with you.'

'Oh, Mack, I can't believe you're here and saying the words I longed so much to hear,' she said, wrapping her arms around him and squeezing him so tightly he grunted. She looked up at him under the shadow of the umbrella. 'I love you too. So much it hurts to be away from you. I've missed you every second we've been apart.'

Mack stroked her face with his free hand. 'I never want to be parted from you again. I know it's a big ask for you to move to Crannochbrae with me. We can commute back and forth so you can keep working in London. I'll buy us a house here. I'll do whatever you want but please say you'll be my wife.'

'Your wife?' Her eyes went out on stalks. 'You're asking me to marry you?'

He smiled so widely it transformed his features. 'Forgive me for not going down on bended knee, but right now there's a river of water running over my feet.'

She glanced down and realised they were standing in a puddle, but she had barely noticed. 'Wow, so there is.'

'How far away is your flat?'

'Just a couple more streets.'

'Good, let's go there so I can do this properly.'

They ran along the footpath, their footsteps splashing as they went. Finally, they came to Elspeth's front door and she quickly unlocked it and they went inside. Mack placed the soaking umbrella in the umbrella stand and smiled. 'Now, where was I?'

'You were about to propose to me on bended knee.'

'Oh, yes, that's right.' He took her hand and then went down on one knee in front of her, his eyes holding hers. He took a familiar-looking velvet box out of his jacket pocket and, deftly flipping it open with one finger, handed her the diamond and sapphire pendant and earrings, but this time, there was a gorgeous engagement ring as well. 'My darling Elspeth, would you do me the very great honour of becoming my wife?'

Elspeth stared at the ring for a long moment, her heart pitter-pattering like the drumming rain outside. 'Oh, Mack…' She dragged him up so he was standing in front of her. 'Of course I will. I love you and want to be with you for ever.'

'Thank goodness for that.' He took the ring out of the box and then, setting the box to one side, slipped the ring on her left hand. She wasn't a bit surprised to find it a perfect fit. 'There. I should have given that to you the first time. I had to fly back to France to get it.'

Elspeth grinned at him. 'Couldn't you have got it posted?'

His eyes were twinkling as bright as the diamond on her hand. 'I wanted to tell the lady who sold me the ensemble she was right. She must have sensed my love for you even before I realised it myself.' He lowered his mouth to hers in a long and loving kiss that sent her senses spinning. She hadn't thought it possible to feel so happy, so overjoyed, so blessed. He finally broke the kiss after some breathless minutes and gazed down at her with adoration shining in his gaze.

'You are everything I could ever want in a life partner. I can't believe I'm so lucky to have found you. And I'm ashamed that I almost lost you out of my stubbornness to admit how much I loved you. I didn't even recognise my own feelings. How stupid is that? When you had that episode of anaphylaxis, I was so terrified of losing you, but I didn't recognise that as love. I insulted you by offering you an extended fling. And you were right to call me out on it. I've wasted so much time not opening up to how I really felt. Time we could have spent planning our wedding.'

Elspeth linked her arms around his neck, gazing up at him in rapture. 'I can't wait to marry you. I didn't realise how much I wanted the fairy tale until I met you. I've spent most of my life hiding away, missing out on the things other people take for granted. But meeting you changed all that and I found I couldn't go back to being happy with my old life. I'd outgrown it. You have made me outgrow it.'

He hugged her close, his expression full of love. 'I'm so glad we found each other. I can't imagine how lonely my life would be without you. You've taught me so much. I'm even playing the piano again.'

'Really?'

'Yes, really. And it was like finding a part of myself I'd lost a long time ago. You gave it back to me, my darling. You taught me how to be whole again.'

Elspeth stroked the lean length of his jaw. 'You taught me things too. I took on board what you said about handling my mother. I now check in with her first thing each day and last thing at night and guess what? She's improved out of sight, and, not only that, she's started seeing someone. She hasn't had a partner since the divorce because she's always been so preoccupied with taking care of me.'

He smiled. 'I'm glad for her and for you. I'm looking forward to meeting her. Do you think she'll approve of your choice of husband?'

'I'm sure she will,' Elspeth said. 'And Elodie will too. I just hope she finds the same happiness one day.'

'That's one of the things I adore about you,' Mack said. 'You're always thinking about others. The way you worried about Sabine at the wedding, for instance. I was so touched by that.'

'I ran into her a few weeks back,' Elspeth said. 'She turned up at my regular lunch spot close to the library. She was lovely about everything. She seems to be coping quite well without Fraser in her life. How is he doing, by the way?'

'Surprisingly well,' Mack said. 'He's enjoying his career and seems determined to turn his life around. I hope you can find it in yourself to forgive him for everything that happened between him and Elodie. I know he can be a bit of a jerk but, this time, I think he's genuinely trying to work on himself. Losing Sabine has made him grow up at long last.'

'Do you think he really loved her?'

Mack shrugged. 'Who knows? But it's too late. Sabine has moved on.'

Elspeth raised her eyebrows. 'Really? You mean she's found someone else? She didn't say anything when we met but, then again, that was weeks ago. I haven't been in touch since.'

'She's dating an old school friend, apparently he was her first boyfriend. It looks serious.'

Elspeth smiled. 'They do say you never forget your first love.'

Mack gathered her close and brought his mouth down to just above hers. 'Especially when they are as unforgettable and adorable as you.' He brushed her lips with a soft kiss and added, 'I think this occasion calls for a bit more Robert Burns, don't you?'

'What did you have in mind?'

His smile was warm and full of devotion as he quoted, *'"But to see her was to love her. Love but her, and love for ever".'* And then his mouth captured hers in a kiss that swept her away on a cloud of happiness.

\* \* \* \* \*

*Enchanted by*
Shy Innocent in the Spotlight?
*Don't miss the next instalment of*
*The Scandalous Campbell Sisters*

*In the meantime, get lost in these*
*other stories by Melanie Milburne!*

His Innocent's Passionate Awakening
One Night on the Virgin's Terms
Breaking the Playboy's Rules
One Hot New York Night
The Billion-Dollar Bride Hunt

*Available now!*